P9-CBQ-652

The UNION CLUB MYSTERIES

ISAAC ASIMOV

FAWCETT CREST • NEW YORK

ACKNOWLEDGMENTS

All the stories in this book were originally published in *Gallery*, in successive monthly issues from September 1980 to February 1983 inclusive.

Copyright © 1980, 1981, 1982, 1983 by Montcalm Publishing Corporation

The titles under which the stories appeared in *Gallery* are given in the following paragraph in parentheses:

NO REFUGE COULD SAVE ("To Spot a Spy"), THE TELEPHONE NUMBER ("The Winning Number"), THE MEN WHO WOULDN'T TALK ("Pigeon English"), A CLEAR SHOT ("Big Shot"), IRRESISTIBLE TO WOMEN ("Call Me Irresistible"), HE WASN'T THERE ("The Spy Who Was Out-of-Focus"), THE THIN LINE ("Taxicab Crackdown"), MYSTERY TUNE ("Death Song"), HIDE AND SEEK ("Hide and Seek"), GIFT ("Decipher Deception"), HOT OR COLD ("Hot or Cold"), THE THIRTEENTH PAGE ("The Thirteenth Page"), 1 TO 999 ("One in a Thousand"), TWELVE YEARS OLD ("The 12-Year-Old Problem"), TESTING, TESTING! ("Cloak and Dagger Duel"), THE APPLEBY STORY ("The Last Laugh"), DOLLARS AND CENTS ("Countdown to Disaster"), FRIENDS AND ALLIES ("Mirror Image"), WHICH IS WHICH? ("The Perfect Alibi"), THE SIGN ("The Telltale Sign"), CATCHING THE FOX ("Stopping the Fox"), GETTING THE COMBINATION ("Playing It by the Numbers"), THE LIBRARY BOOK ("Mystery Book"), THE THREE GOBLETS ("A Flash of Brilliance"), SPELL IT! ("Book Smart"), TWO WOMEN ("Cherchez la Femme: The Case of the Disappearing Woman"), SENDING A SIGNAL ("A Piece of the Rock"), THE FAVORITE PIECE ("Face the Music"), HALF A GHOST ("A Ghost of a Chance"), THERE WAS A YOUNG LADY ("Poetic License")

A Fawcett Crest Book
Published by Ballantine Books

Library of Congress Catalog Card Number: 82-45974

ISBN 0-449-20525-8

This edition published by arrangement with Doubleday & Company, Inc.

Printed in Canada

First Ballantine Books Edition: February 1985

Dedicated to Eric Protter
who said, "Would you?"

Foreword

Three years ago (as I write this) Eric Protter of *Gallery* magazine asked me if I would consider writing a monthly mystery for the magazine.

I hesitated. *Gallery* is what is commonly known as a "girlie" magazine and, like all of that genre, though not as tastelessly as some, it is devoted to the feminine form divine—and unclothed. I have no objection to that in principle, you understand, and I have written articles for *Gallery* and for a few other magazines of the sort. After all, no one compels me to read anything of which I disapprove, even if something of mine appears in the issue. I can always take out the pages on which my article appears and bind them along with other such tear sheets, and discard the rest of the magazine if I wish. And if a revealing photograph should appear on the other side of a page containing part of my article—well, I don't have to look.—And if I do, I'll survive. (I'm sure of it.)

The articles, however, were always on scientific subjects. I had never been asked to write fiction before.

So after I was finished hesitating, I said cautiously, "Eric, you understand, I hope, that I do not write erotica." (I don't! Just a silly idiosyncrasy of mine! I write an occasional ribald limerick, but that's just for laughs.)

Eric said, "I know that. I just want a mystery written in *your* style. I want it about two thousand words long, and I want you to stop toward the end so that the reader will have a chance to solve the mystery before your detective does. We will publish the end of the story on another page."

I found that notion intriguing. The first story was satisfactory, but, as it turned out, I hadn't quite gotten into my stride. It was with my second story, "No Refuge Could Save," that I worked out my scheme.

Since I am always fair with my readers I will tell you what it is. Each story (without exception) starts with a short exchange among three cronies in the library of the Union Club. The fourth crony is Griswold, who is asleep as the story starts. Something in the exchange stirs him awake and reminds him of a story, which he tells up to the point where the other three ought to be able to solve the mystery. They never do, and Griswold gives them the answer.

When Griswold comes to the end of his story, you will find a typographical intimation of that fact, and you will be welcome to try to guess the ending before going on. There may be times when the ending will be obvious to you. There may be times when you'll decide (with indignation) that no human being could have solved the puzzle given only the information I deigned to hand out. There may be times when you will think, in hindsight, that you ought to have guessed it, and will applaud my cleverness in concealing the answer without being unfair about it. And you may well decide the heck with trying to guess the answer, and just read on to the end.

But however it goes, I can only hope that a good number of the stories will interest and amuse you, and that you won't be sorry you invested in this book.

One last word of warning. I have the trick of sounding as though I know all sorts of inside things about spies and police departments and government operations. If you're curious, the truth is I don't know a *thing* about any of that sort of stuff. I make it all up in my head, and if you should be an expert and should note that I am ludicrously wrong in some ways—that's why!

Contents

The UNION CLUB
CLUB
MYSTERIES

No Refuge Could Save

When we four sat in the Union Club on a snowy evening, the talk was always most relaxed when Griswold was sleeping. That was when we knew the conversational ball would bounce most efficiently.

Baranov said, "What I don't understand about this rash of spy stories infesting us today is what the hell spies are good for nowadays. We have spy satellites that tell us just about everything."

"Absolutely right," said Jennings. "Besides, what secrets are there anymore? If you explode a nuclear test bomb, monitors pick it up. We've got every enemy installation keyed in to a missile all set to go and so do they. Our computers hold off their computers and vice versa."

"It's all very boring in real life," I said, "but I suppose the books make money."

Griswold's eyes were tightly shut. From the fact that his fourth scotch and soda was firmly in his hand, nearly full, we might suppose he wasn't sleeping or he would spill it—but that didn't follow. We had heard him snore for an hour and a half at a time and never spill a full glass. He would hold a glass firmly if the rest of him were palsied.

We were wrong this time, though. He was awake. His eyes opened and he said, "The trouble is you don't know anything about spies. Nobody does." And he raised his glass to sip at it.

"Even spies know nothing about spies," he said—

* * *

I wasn't exactly a spy during World War II [said Griswold], at least in my own evaluation of the matter.

No beautiful woman sought me out in terror and asked me to take charge of a microfilm at the risk of my life. I was never pursued up and over the Statue of Liberty or the Golden Gate Bridge by sinister villains with Lugers in their overcoat pockets. I was never sent behind enemy lines in order to blow up a key installation.

As a matter of fact, I was a youngster in my early twenties who sat around a Philadelphia laboratory and wondered why it was that the draft never seemed to touch me. When I tried to volunteer, I was thrown out of the recruiting office. When I tried to talk to my draft board, I was told they were all out of town.

It was many years later that I decided I was kept in civilian life because of my duties as a spy.

You see, the thing about spies that most people don't know is that none of them really know what they're doing. They can't know; it wouldn't be safe for them to know. As soon as a spy knows too much, he can hurt the cause if he's taken. If a spy knows too much, he becomes valuable and he can be tempted to defect, or to get drunk and talk, or to meet some glamorous woman and end up whispering in her ear.

A spy is safe only when he is ignorant. He is safest when he doesn't even know he's a spy.

Somewhere deep in the Pentagon, or the White House, or some brownstone in Nyack or San Antonio or wherever, there are spy masters who know enough to be important; but no one knows who they are, and I shouldn't be surprised if, in the end, none of them knew it all either.

That's why there are so many idiot mistakes in wars. Everyone without exception has areas of darkness, because too much light would make them each untrustworthy and generals have a talent for choosing areas of darkness in which to operate.

Read your military history, gentlemen, and see if that doesn't make sense out of a lot of the madness.

Well, I was a spy. I was just a kid, so I was in the lowest echelon, which meant I knew nothing at all. I just got my orders, but I thought they just involved my work in the lab. Of course I was a bright kid—as you will not be surprised to hear, gentlemen—and I usually got results. That made me valuable.

Naturally, I didn't realize this at the time or I would have asked for a raise in pay. After all, $2,600 a year wasn't much even in those times. I guess that was another reason they kept me in ignorance. It meant they could economize.

Looking back on it years later, though, I remember one little feat of mine that should have gotten me a thousand-dollar raise—or a Congressional Medal of Honor—whichever was better.

I'll have to do a little explaining.

We were fighting the Germans in those days, you might remember. We were also fighting the Japanese, but I was out of that. I didn't have the eyes for work among the Orientals.

Now the Germans were efficient. They infiltrated us, you know. They sent any number of men into the United States. They sent those men with false identities, false papers, false histories. They did a wonderful and thorough job.

You might ask, couldn't we do the same and send Americans into Germany?

Sure we could, but we never had a chance. The Germans had a pretty homogeneous society and we didn't. We are a melting pot. We've got all kinds of accents here and all kinds of ethnicities.

If one of our agents made some small error in Germany, they'd have him strung up by the thumbs before he was quite finished with the error. Over here, we've got to wait for ten or twelve months before we're sure whether someone's a German agent or an honest and loyal Mitteleuropean-American or something.

So we were always running behind. Naturally, I knew nothing of this. No one did except maybe five people who knew 25 percent apiece. I know that comes to a total of 125 percent, but there was some overlapping.

My talent was that I could spot phonies. That's what

kept me out of the army. They needed that old infallible spotter—me.

So when they had some true-blue American who had perpetrated what might be (or what might not be) a floater, I was put on him. They'd call me in and tell me they wanted to hire someone to work at the Naval Air Experimental Station, where I worked as a chemist, and they weren't sure about his loyalty.

I didn't think much of it. We had a lieutenant commander who suspected anyone who knew any two-syllable words, and whoever it was always turned out to be an honest, decent, income-tax-cheating, draft-dodging American. Except sometimes.

This time I was called in to the commanding officer's office. I didn't know why. Much later, I came across some papers that made it look as though the incident involved something that meant victory or defeat in the war. I haven't the faintest idea why, but the war would surely have been lost if I didn't come through.

Naturally, I didn't know it at the time.

"Griswold," said the commander, "we've got a new man. His name is Brooke. He spells his name with an 'e.' We're not sure about him. He may be a true-blue American. He may be a sneaking, stinking Nazi. You find out for us and don't let him know you're finding out, because we don't want him on his guard. What's more, Griswold, we've got to know by 5 P.M. and we've got to know it right. If you come up with no answer by 5 P.M. or with the wrong answer, well, Griswold—"

He lit up his cigarette, stared at me, narrow-eyed through the smoke, and said in a voice that would have chipped granite, "If you fail, Griswold, you can forget about any promotions."

That *really* put the pressure on me. If I had known the course of the war was at stake, I could have shrugged it off. Losing a war is just an item in history, but losing a promotion is a personal tragedy.

I looked at my watch. It was 10:15 A.M., which would have given me nearly seven hours.

I didn't get to meet him for half an hour; and then one

of the lab managers felt it incumbent to spend two hours explaining the new man's duties to him.

It wasn't till nearly 2 P.M. that we found ourselves at adjacent lab desks, and I could really strike up a conversation with him.

He was a very pleasant fellow, which was a mark against him, of course, because a secret agent tries to be pleasant. The trouble is that so do a certain percentage of loyal people—not many, but enough do so to confuse the issue.

I assumed he wouldn't mind a little gentle probing. He would expect it and he would be bound to cooperate.

For one thing, if he held back, that would be suspicious. If he were an enemy agent, reserve might attract attention to him and he would be shot. If he were not an enemy agent, reserve might indicate stupidity and he might be promoted into an administrative position. Both eventualities were equally undesirable.

Besides this, German agents sent to infiltrate defense agencies inside the United States tended to glory in their ability to withstand probing, and they seemed to invite questions.

After all, they were chosen from those who had spent their early years in the United States, so that they could easily slip back into American idiomatic English, and, in addition, they were thoroughly grounded in American trivia.

For instance, you've all heard that the way to tell a German spy who's pretending to be an American is to ask him who won the World Series the year before. Don't you believe it! Every single one of them is thoroughly up on the World Series and on all the baseball statistics, to say nothing of prizefighting and the name of every Vice-President for the last fifty years.

But there had to be some way.

I talked politics and sports with him and he knew as much as I did about them. I tried all kinds of idioms and slang expressions on him and they never fazed him.

Fortunately, we were both involved with reflux condensations on our desks, which gave us plenty of time to talk. Besides, in civil service jobs, undue attention to one's work is considered highly suspicious, especially in wartime.

I suggested word games, therefore, and we played a few harmless ones, and then by easy stages we got to free association. I told him that I would bet that no matter how he tried to mask the fact, I could by free associations tell him the last time he had been to bed with a girl friend and exactly what they had done. We had a five-dollar bet on it and an additional five dollars he wouldn't answer each word or phrase within five seconds by my watch.

It was 4:20 P.M. when we started and you can bet we were both serious. We were fighting for victory in war and for ten dollars, and both of us thought a lot of ten dollars.

I said "table" and he said "bed"; I said "DiMaggio" and he said "homerun"; I said "G.I." and he said "Joe"; I said "clarinet" and he said "Benny Goodman." It went on like that for quite a while, with me slowly getting more complicated by delicate little stages.

Finally at 4:45 P.M. I said "terror of flight" and he said "gloom of the grave" and I gave an agreed-upon signal and a fellow sitting at a desk at the other end of the room stood up, walked over, collared the guy and took off. He kept yelling "You owe me ten bucks" all the way out, but I can tell you he had a fat chance of collecting.

From what I told you, I suppose you can see what happened, so if you don't mind, I'll just catch up on the remaining twenty of my forty winks.

We had to wake him. "What happened?" I said, shaking him rather roughly, so that he was hard put to it to hold his scotch and soda steady. "Finish the damn story."

"You mean you don't get it?" he said indignantly. "Terror of flight' is from the third stanza of 'The Star-Spangled Banner,' which goes:

And where is that band who so vauntingly swore
That the havoc of war and the battle's confusion
A home and a country should leave us no more?

Their blood has washed out their foul footsteps' pollution.
No refuge could save the hireling and slave
From the terror of flight, or the gloom of the grave:
And the star-spangled banner in triumph doth wave
O'er the land of the free and the home of the brave!

"Well, damn it, gentlemen, no loyal, true-blue American knows the words of the first stanza of our glorious national anthem, and they've never even heard of the third stanza (except for me, of course, since I know everything). In any case, the third stanza is chauvinist and bloody-minded and it was practically read out of the anthem during the great peace-loving days of World War II.

"It's just that the Germans are so thorough they carefully taught their agents all four verses of the anthem and made sure they had them down letter-perfect—and that was the dead giveaway.

"The only trouble was that the commander never did give me my raise and they didn't even reimburse me for the ten-dollar bet I lost."

I said, "But you never paid the ten dollars."

"Yes," said Griswold, "but they didn't know that." And he fell asleep again.

The Telephone Number

"I'm a corporation now," said Jennings, with a kind of dubious pride, "but what it means is that I've got an employer's identification number now that I must remember. That's on top of my social security number and telephone number and zip code and my car's license plate."

"And your address, and the combination of any combination lock you might have," said Baranov even more gloomily, "and the birthdays and anniversaries of all your relatives and friends. We're prisoners of a numbered society."

"That," said I, "is the reason why we need to be computerized. Feed all the numbers into a computer and let *it* do the worrying."

At which Griswold stirred. His chair creaked defiantly as he leaned forward, puffed out his white mustache, and stared at us balefully.

"I'm not much good at remembering numbers," he said, "but I knew a man once who never forgot one."

He paused to sip at the scotch and soda he seems always to be holding, but there was no danger we would get away. There's something in the way Griswold looks at you through vaguely bloodshot eyes that forces you into a verbal paralysis.

His name was Bulmerson [said Griswold] and those were the days when we were holed up in a little room at the Pentagon, which nobody could find except Bulmerson and me, and two or three others who worked with us.

There was a sort of shabby linen-closet look about the room and it had a sign on the door that had nothing to do with what went on inside. I doubt that there were five men outside our group who knew what we were up to, and that goes even for the upper-echelon Pentagon personnel.

I remember an admiral once wandering in under the impression he was visiting a men's room. He kept looking vaguely around for the urinals as though he were sure we had one of them hidden in the lockers. We had to lead him out gently.

What was going on, of course, was intelligence. Not James Bond heroics. Infinitely duller. Infinitely more important. It was just a matter of weighing information and deciding whether it was reliable or not, and just how one piece of news fit with another, and to what degree it was possible that someone who said "yes" really meant "no" or vice versa.

After doing all that we had to be ready to advise the President or the State Department and sweat out the result. We earned our money, actually—not that we were paid very much.

Bulmerson had been at it longest. A big man, broad, white hair, always very red in the face, thick neck and bulging at every seam. Looked as though he should be smoking a cigar, but he didn't.

It was he who never forgot a number. He knew the telephone number of a thousand officials and ten thousand nonofficials and never got them wrong. He could manage other kinds of numbers as well, but telephone numbers were his particular hobby. I think his secret ambition was to replace the telephone book.

It might have been that little quirk in his head that made it possible for him to have the sixth sense for telling when some foreign statesman had broken down and forgetfully said something that wasn't a lie. Who knows how odd talents fit together. Maybe it was his number sense that somehow made him an infallible spotter of the infrequent truth, and that was always valuable. He was much looked up to, was Bulmerson.

Then, too, all sorts of raw data came to us. Any anonymous phone tip was routed to us. We don't know the motives that make people report to us. We just make use of it—if we dare. Sometimes the bits we get are from harmless lunatics and sometimes from enemy agents who are making a definite attempt to mislead us. Winnowing out the ounce of wheat from the ton of chaff is another one of our jobs.

We had one informer who was infallible, though. He had found *us,* for one thing, and that was impressive. He called us directly and we never found out how he had discovered how to reach us. He was always right.

We never found out who he was, though. His voice was soft and hoarse and seemed vaguely non-American. We called him Our Boy. If it had happened a dozen years later we might have called him Deep Throat. This was in the early 1960s, however.

We made no attempt to locate him or identify him, because we feared that anything we did might stop him and we didn't want him stopped. He was our keyhole into the Kremlin. After 1965, we never heard from him again. He may have been shifted out of the country or he might have died—even naturally, for all we know. But this was a couple of years earlier.

He called, but it was always in a special way. First someone else would call and give us a telephone number and time limits. If we used that telephone number at the particular time, we got *him*. We had a little code phrase to identify each other, and then he would talk for a minute or two and hang up. We always acted on what he said and we were never sorry we did.

The numbers were always pay phones (we did check that much), but we didn't know what system he used to pick them out, for, of course, he never used the same one twice. For that matter, he never seemed to use the same person twice for making the initial call. We don't know how he picked them. They may have been winos he bought for a bottle for the one job. You can't smell their breath over the telephone.

Bulmerson always enjoyed it when he happened to

pick up the telephone at the time when the message was a telephone number and a time from Our Boy. The rest of us had to scribble the number down and sometimes even say, "Would you repeat that, please?"

In that case, Bulmerson would be insufferable the rest of the day, and comment on premature senility. He was very childish about it.

Of course, when *he* answered the phone, he just listened and then hung up without saying a word. Then, when the time came, he would just call, having made no note but having filed the number in his capacious and infallible number memory.

It was just two months before the assassination of President Kennedy—

I was in the office with Bulmerson, who wasn't looking particularly well, and with two others— What were their names? I don't remember, but it doesn't matter. Call them Smith and Jones.

It was a muggy day, overcast and gloomy, not at all comfortable even though it was just about the autumnal equinox that supposedly ends summer. In the Washington area, summer doesn't end as neatly as that, or on time.

Bulmerson was scowling because he said the lousy sandwich he'd had for lunch had left him with heartburn, and that didn't strike me as odd considering the trouble we were having in Vietnam.

Ngo Dinh Diem was running South Vietnam pretty much to suit himself, and his way of doing so wasn't suiting *us*. He was growing increasingly unpopular and Buddhist monks were burning themselves alive in protest, which they were not doing in North Vietnam and which made our side look like the villains. What's more, the number of American "advisers" was rising steadily and had passed the ten-thousand mark.

It was clear, at least to the little group of us whose job it was to study the world of international politics, that we were being suckered into a booby trap, but it didn't seem as if there were anything that could be done about it. We couldn't leave and make it look as though we were abandoning an ally, and the Democrats, in particular, would have been skinned alive if they had— But you all know the story—

What we needed was some way of getting a clean-cut, fairly bloodless, and quick—especially quick—victory, and get out. What happened afterward, well, at least it would happen without Americans in the middle of it. Trouble was we didn't have that way.

Then, on the day I'm talking about, the telephone rang and it was Bulmerson, scowling, who picked it up.

"Adamson's Five and Ten," he said, that being the code phrase of the day.

He listened expressionlessly, then hung up the telephone without saying a word.

He turned to us, gasping a little, and said, "Our Boy wants to talk to us and it's got to be in thirty minutes, between 2:30 P.M. and 2:35, and it's double-Z."

That was the term Our Boy used when it was highest possible priority. The last time he had used it was during the Cuban missile crisis the previous year, and it had meant we went into it knowing we would win, which was very convenient—and another story.

I said, "Don't forget the telephone number."

A look of contempt crossed Bulmerson's sweating face. "Are you kidding? It's so simple it's no fun to remember it. Even *you* could remember it. At least today you could. I'll even tell you what it is and you'll see. It's 9—"

That's all he said, because he then made a sound that was half gasp, half groan, clutched at his chest and fell to the ground, where he twisted and twitched. That was no heartburn he had been suffering from: it was a coronary and a bad one.

There was nothing we could do except ring Emergency.

I'll say this for the Pentagon. They had a team there in five minutes and the paramedics worked on him for a while, then heaved him into a stretcher and carted him off. It didn't do much good; the poor man died in the hospital that evening.

We remained behind, shocked and stunned, after Bulmerson had been taken away. It's hard to get your bearings when something like that happens.

But then Smith nudged me. He looked pasty white and it wasn't from what he had just seen. He said to me, "Bulmerson never told us the telephone number."

We had to think about that. In our business, it's first things first.

I looked at the clock. It was 2:31 and we had four minutes to go. "Don't worry about it," I said. "He told us enough."

I called and got Our Boy. What he had to say was what we had been waiting to hear. There was a way of getting the Chinese People's Republic into a neat corner. It would take time, but if we played our part correctly, North Vietnam would be unable to move, and we would have the perfect excuse to call it a victory and get out of South Vietnam.

Happy ending—except that things broke wrong. On November 1, Diem was killed in a coup and on November 22, John F. Kennedy was assassinated, and by the time we had the government working again, the chance had passed and there was no way out. Johnson had to keep raising the ante and raising, and, in the end—well, you know the end.

And since I expect you know what the telephone number was, that's the end of the story.

Griswold was closing his eyes, but all three of us were at him simultaneously. Baranov said, "What was the telephone number, and how did you know?"

Griswold raised his white eyebrows. "But it's obvious. Bulmerson said it was an easy number to remember and had time to give the first digit as 9. That meant it could be 999-9999 or 987-6543, which would be the limit he would expect us to be able to keep in mind. He said, however, 'At least today you could.' That made the day special, and what can possibly make a day special in connection with a number but its date.

"I told you it was two months before the assassination,

14

which was on November 22, so the date was September 22, or, if you wish, 22 September. September is the ninth month, so the day can be written 9-22, or 22-9. Bulmerson said the first digit was 9 so, if you forget the hyphen, it was 922. If you remember the year of the assassination, you know the date was 922-1963 and that was the number I dialed.''

The Men Who Wouldn't Talk

"It always puzzled me," said Baranov one night at the Union Club "why, in war, one doesn't strike for the top. Why fight the armies, instead of the man who inspires and leads them. If Napoleon had died early in the game, or Lenin, or Hitler, or, for that matter, Washington—"

Jennings said, "I suppose it's partly a matter of tight security and partly the freemasonry of command. If the leader of government A orders a strike at the leader of government B, he's asking for it himself, isn't he?"

I said, "I think that's overromantic. My feeling is that if a leader dies, someone takes his place who may be even more effective. Philip of Macedon was knocked off before he could invade Persia, but who took his place? His son, who turned out to be Alexander the Great."

Griswold, as usual, was drowsing with his scotch and soda in his hand and, also as usual, managed to hear us just the same. He opened one eye and said, "Sometimes you don't know who the leaders are. Then what do you do?" He opened the other eye and stared at us from under his shaggy eyebrows.

George Plumb [said Griswold] was a penologist who had an interesting theory on the subject of prison management. The problem, he said, was that American prisons fell between two extremes, and uncomfortably so.

Many elements of American society feel prisoners should be treated humanely, with an eye to rehabilitation rather than torture, Many other elements in society feel that prisoners are behind bars in order to be punished and that imprisonment is not, in itself, punishment enough.

The result is an uneasy compromise in that prisoners are generally not treated well enough to keep them from feeling a rising resentment, and, on the other hand, are not treated so badly as to be starved and beaten into helpless compliance. The result is occasional prison riots—as we all know.

Given all this, my friend, Plumb pointed out that riots do not occur predictably. If you follow the misery or cruelty inflicted upon prisoners, you do *not* find that at a certain level, a riot breaks out. In one prison, quite abysmal conditions are endured with nothing more than growls, mutters and an occasional clash of aluminum mugs against iron bars. In other prisons, where conditions are substantially less intolerable, a fierce insurrection will break out.

Plumb insisted it was a matter of leadership. If, in a particular prison there were a prisoner skilled enough or charismatic enough, he could direct the strategy and tactics of a revolt and might even deliberately stir one up where none would otherwise take place.

One must, therefore, Plumb would say, learn to recognize the leader, the man who is clearly respected, or admired, or feared by the prisoners generally and, while matters are as yet quiet, transfer him to another prison. The prison which he has left then remains quiet because the prisoners are without a head and it will take time for another to arise. The prison which he enters does not know him and it will take time for him to rise to a position of leadership.

Plumb's advice was taken on a number of occasions and, if the transfer were followed by at least some improvement in prisoner treatment, riots were invariably aborted.

Some years ago, at one particular prison—it wouldn't be wise to mention its name—conditions for a riot seemed to be mounting. The prison guards reported a dangerous restlessness among the inmates, a clear spirit of rebellion.

Plumb was called in and, of course, his first question

was for the name of the prisoners' leader. He was astonished when the prison officials, from the warden down, professed complete ignorance on the subject. There was no one prisoner who was clearly at the head.

"There must be one," said Plumb. "A mob doesn't move by general consent. Someone has to shout, 'What are we waiting for? Let's go!' "

There was a collective shaking of heads. If there was a leader, he had cannily kept such a low profile he was unrecognized.

Plumb, deeply worried, came to me. He knew me well enough to know that no one could help him, if I couldn't.

He said, "Griswold, I have a master criminal here, the kind who is so skilled that his machinations are invisible. How do I identify him out of three thousand or so inmates?"

I said, "The prison authorities may not know who he is, but at least some of the prisoners must. Question the prisoners."

He favored me with a look of contempt. "That won't be any help at all. Prisoners are men who wouldn't talk, and you know that. We all have a code against snitching, and criminals, in particular, are strong on that. It is their one sure homage to virtue. They may kill, steal or rape; but they are not so lost to shame and decency as to be tattletales.

"Besides," he went on, "each prisoner has to live with the rest of them. Anyone known to have cooperated with the authorities, anyone *suspected* of having cooperated with the authorities, can expect nothing less than constant sadistic mistreatment from the prisoners generally—possibly he may be killed by them."

I said, "You've got to choose the right one, Plumb. There's such a thing as a leader, and there's also such a thing as a nonfollower: someone who stands out against the crowd even when it's dangerous to do so."

Plumb said, "Not that much danger. The oddball will be the first one suspected. Even if we promise to transfer him, he'll be sure that the grapevine will carry the news to the new prison. And if we promise to get him out of prison altogether, he might well be afraid he wouldn't be safe from revenge even then."

I could see that there was something to that, but I said, "Just the same, consult the warden and find out if there's someone in the prison who is an intellectual, is afraid of violence, has a horror of the other prisoners, and who expects to get out soon. If he works in the library and therefore feels superior to the other prisoners, so much the better."

Plumb said, "Even if I found such a man, I couldn't use him. If I questioned him in privacy, the prisoners might not know what he said, but they will suspect he lacks the guts to resist. They will haze him afterward and if we should get our man, even if it were for reasons that had nothing to do with your intellectual, they would still kill him."

I said, "You don't call him alone. Call a hundred men, a thousand, as many as you can handle. Call him somewhere in the middle. Let him know you're asking every person in the prison and he just might work up the courage to give you your lead."

Plumb came to see me again about ten days later. He looked as though he could use some sleep badly.

He said, and his voice was a little hoarse, "We went through about half the prisoners, concentrating on the long-termers and the tough guys, but we deliberately called in some of the older men and the cream puffs. No one would talk. You never saw such a mass of concentrated ignorance in your life, but of course it was only what I expected—and meanwhile conditions are growing more tense. The guards are on the alert, but I have a feeling that this mysterious leader, whoever he may be, who is shrewd enough to remain unknown, is also shrewd enough to counter and beat any defense the warden may put up. And we can't just lock everyone in the cells, remove all clothing, throw fifty men we like the least into solitary, and do it all just on suspicion. The cries of 'prison brutality' that would arise—" He shuddered.

I said, "Did you find a prisoner of the type I suggested?"

"Yes, I did," he said. "*Exactly.* He'll be out in six months; he's a stranger to violence and is in for business fraud. He shouldn't even be in this particular prison. He speaks well, and is well educated. He works in the library, and he is clearly embarrassed and humiliated at being in prison and, even more, at having to associate with the prisoners.''

"And what did he say, Plumb?"

"Say? Nothing! I don't even think it was a case of being scared. I think he really didn't know. Why should he? He stays away from the prisoners as much as he can. Personally, I think he has built a little world of his own in which he pretends he's alone.''

I said, "Is he intelligent?"

"Oh, yes," said Plumb. "I should say very intelligent. He spends most of his time in the library, reading.''

"Then it seems to me he's got to know."

"What am I supposed to do? Beat it out of him? These days we can't touch them.''

"He must know that the last thing he wants is a prison riot with all its dangers. Surely, he would want to do anything to stop it. He must have tried to get something across. Tell me, Plumb, do you remember exactly what he said to you?''

"Griswold," said Plumb wearily, "we've carefully recorded all the proceedings. As it happens, however, it is very easy to tell you what he said to us. He told us nothing—blank—zero.''

I said, "Do you mean that he told you he didn't know anything? Or did he say nothing at all and just sit there in silence?''

Plumb said, "For the most part he just sat there in silence. He was a little fellow, thin, a small prissy mouth, narrow chin, pale eyes, and he just looked at me with his knees together and his hands clasped in his lap and a faraway look in his eyes. Not a word, till just at the end.''

"Ah, what did he say at the end?"

"I was exasperated. I asked him if he heard me at all, if he understood what I was saying. Then his eyes flickered in my direction. There was a ghost of a smile on his face and he said, 'No, I haven't. It—was—Greek—to—me.' He spaced the words as though in deliberate insolence and I just ached to punch him in the nose. But I let him go. What else could I do?"

I said, "You recorded all the interviews. Do you suppose the recordings, or their contents, could leak out to the prisoners?".

"They shouldn't, but—" Plumb shrugged.

"They probably will. And our man was very clever. If the rest got the records and found out what he had said, they would consider him a regular guy and a hero. They would have no way of knowing that he gave us the answer."

Plumb looked astonished. "He *did*?"

"I think so. I can't be sure at the moment, but I think so. Do you have a roster of the prisoners?"

I was given one the next day and picked out the one I thought it might be in less than five minutes. He was transferred and there was no riot. Our friend the prison librarian was released six months later and was then quietly pardoned and his prison record erased.

Griswold freshened his scotch and then allowed his eyes to close.

Baranov leaned over and quietly removed the glass of scotch from Griswold's hand. His eyes opened at once, and he said, "Hey, put that drink back."

"First," said Baranov, "how did you find out who the riot leader was?"

Griswold said, "Oh, you didn't get it? You surprise me! The librarian said, 'It was Greek to me' with emphasis. He was a reader, and it so happens the expression is a quotation. It is *not* an age-old common saying whose origins are lost in mystery. The phrase is Shakespeare's, no less, and is to be found in the play *Julius Caesar*. One of the conspirators describes a political rally at which Cicero spoke in Greek. When asked what Cicero had said, the character said he didn't know, adding, 'those that understood him smil'd at one another and shook their heads; but for mine own part, it was Greek to me.' "

"So?" asked Jennings.

"So, the conspirator who made that statement in the

play was Casca, and it occurred to me that if I looked through the roster of prisoners' names, I might find one that resembled Casca, or, possibly, Cicero. On the roster was one Benny W. Kasker who, I was told upon inquiry, was intelligent, unscrupulous and in for life. I felt that he might very well be the one—and he was.''

A Clear Shot

I suppose everyone talks about terrorism these days, even in the august and untouchable interior of the Union Club. It was not really a surprise, then, that Jennings went on for some five emotional minutes about the dangers we all ran because there was no rational pattern to terrorist attacks.

Baranov said, finally, when Jennings ran down, "Come, come, old man. Lightning does not strike the valleys. Not one of us is important enough to make a fair target."

"Sometimes they're chosen at random," I said. "That's Jennings's point."

Baranov snorted. "Automobile accidents can strike at anyone, too, but I don't notice people going into blue funks over it. You just do your best."

It was at this moment that Griswold stirred. The first sign was the clinking of the ice in his scotch and soda, and then he opened one eye and puffed out his magnificent white mustache.

"It may be," he said, "that lightning doesn't strike the valleys" (It always amazed us that he heard every word we said even when he was sound asleep, or appeared to be.) "and you three may be safe, but I was the subject of a terrorist threat at one time. It was back in 1969—"

I quickly said, "I believe they're featuring poached salmon for dinner tonight—" but both of Griswold's eyes were open now and they pinned us to the wall like blue icicles.

*   *   *

It was back in 1969 [said Griswold], and that was a bad year for prominent Americans. Robert Kennedy and Martin Luther King, Jr. had been gunned down not long before, and I rather suspected I might be next. I had been engaged in matters I am still not at liberty to discuss, but, of course, secrets are never absolute, and I had made enemies.

Add to that the unrest on American campuses and anyone could clearly see that matters were rising to a scream. In May of that year, I was up for an honorary degree at a college in Connecticut—I forget the name, for all that nonsense seems to melt together in my mind, but I believe the degree that time was a doctorate in Humane Letters.

Two days before the ceremony, however, the president of the college received an anonymous communication to the effect that my honorary degree must be canceled forthwith because of my nefarious activities in Vietnam. If it were not canceled and if I appeared at the commencement, I would be killed. The letter said, for I remember the exact words, "If the commencement features this monster, nothing will prevent me from getting him in my sights and getting off a clear shot."

Still, the person making the threat claimed to be as humane as the Letters with which I was to be honored, for he assured the president that no one else would be harmed, which was, of course, little consolation for me.

The president had showed me the letter at once, in strictest privacy, and asked if I wished to avoid the confrontation. I could plead illness and the degree would be granted to me in absentia. The diploma could then be mailed to me.

It was clear to me that it was the president who wished to avoid the confrontation, and that encouraged all that was quixotic in me. If he was going to play the coward, I was not.

Besides, why should I be deprived of my moment of glory, microscopic though it was? In the first place, I had done nothing in Vietnam to warrant indignation. My mission there had been a cover for the actual work I was doing in the Middle East in the wake of the Six-Day War.

Besides, I did not think the letter had to be taken seriously. I said so. I told the president rather huffily that I would not give in to bluff.

"Bluff?" he said nervously. "How can you be sure it's bluff?"

"Because he announced it, sir," I thundered. "You don't suppose Lee Harvey Oswald or Sirhan Sirhan sent little billets-doux warning their victims, do you? The writer of this note merely wants to disrupt the commencement and humiliate me—and I have no intention of cooperating."

The president shook his head. "But we can't simply assume it's a hoax of some sort. Suppose we ignored this, took no precautions—and you were then shot. And suppose the existence of this note were then to become known. My position—"

"—would not be as uncomfortable as mine," I said with heavy irony. "If I'm willing to chance it, why not you?"

"Because my responsibility is to the college and not to myself, my dear sir. This letter may have been sent on impulse, but if we ignore it, his pride may be as great as yours and he may be forced to make the attempt even if he doesn't really want to."

For a moment I considered the situation and thought I understood it. But then—I might be wrong. "Very well," I said. "Take the necessary precautions."

"But my dear Mr. Griswold," he said, "that would scarcely do. Surely, it would be just as disruptive of the commencement if I were to litter the place with guards and search all the students, parents and friends for concealed weapons—something that would in any case slow the proceedings intolerably. It would be the better part of valor to—"

"Nonsense," I said. "Half the college commencements this year are being disrupted one way or another. The presence of guards would seem a natural precaution and would probably titillate the audience. If you really think someone intends to smuggle a high-powered rifle with a telescopic lens into the stands, your task is simple. Such a weapon is not easily masked. Just have the guards watch for long boxes, suspicious canes, crutches, fishing rods, or anything long and narrow. It would have to be in plain view, for Sunday is forecast as a hot day and anyone wearing an outer garment will be at once suspicious.''

The president said, ''The graduating class will wear flowing academic robes—''

''But they will walk in procession and anyone with a rifle under his robes will surely walk stiffly. That goes for the faculty, including you and me. And if you're going to mention the band, you can easily check out their instrument cases and make sure they contain only instruments.''

In short, I overbore him. I didn't for a moment think a rifle could be smuggled into the field, or aimed if it were, and I thought I knew what ought to be done. But let the president go through the motions, I thought. It would be a useful diversion perhaps and then, as I said before—I might be wrong.

I walked out onto the field at the tail of the procession with the president on my right side, two days later. It was a hot and beautiful day, as had been forecast, and the students in their black caps and gowns were standing at their seats. The stands were full of happy people, making a complex patchwork of color. Hundreds of amateur cameramen hovered at the fringes, hoping to catch the young hopefuls at the moment of diploma presentation or snapping the academic procession. A few even took photos of me, lured, I suppose, by the majesty of my countenance.

The president, I couldn't help but notice, left an unusually large gap between us. He was thinking, I know, of someone with a rifle and he didn't want to become the well-known innocent bystander.

From the platform, I looked over the audience. I was more than ever confident that no one would shoot from the stands, or succeed in getting 'a clear shot,' as he called it, if he tried. If someone tried to aim a rifle, it would have to be from some secluded spot where the aiming could be in leisurely and uninterrupted tranquillity—as in Oswald's case.

I looked for windows that overlooked the platform, but there were none. The platform was blocked off behind and above and, to some extent, on the sides. Before us were the people out to the wall of the stadium and beyond that nothing but blue sky.

In the foreground there were marshals and photographers and newspapermen introducing a note of scurry and incoherence. That was all right, for one of the photographers was really one of my men who knew what to watch for, and whom I didn't want noticed. And somewhere around the stands were the guards whom the president had set up and whom *I* had not noticed.

The president spoke; a minister invoked the blessing of the deity; one of the students gave a short speech in an embarrassed tone; then I rose while the president read an encomium that was supposed to justify my honorary degree. With the adjectives done, a hood was placed over my head and all retreated from me, leaving me alone at the podium to give my twenty-minute address.

This was it. If the prospective assassin were really serious about killing me, and if he were also serious about doing no harm to anyone else, this was the time. I was alone—or at least more alone than anyone else would be at any time during the ceremonies. There were twenty others on the platform, but they were well behind me and were sitting down. A bullet that was fired at my head, for instance, would strike nothing if it missed me.

And I would have to count on the miss now or, better yet, on stopping the act before it could be performed.

The manuscript with my speech was in front of me, but I was going to have to improvise, for I was going to have to watch what went on before me. I couldn't help but sweep the stands as I began my address, but that was foolish. I was not likely to make out anything important at that distance and by the time I heard the crack of the rifle across the field the bullet would be in me.

Leave that part to the guards! I would concentrate on what went on immediately before me. I trusted my friend, whom I noticed at one side, but two sets of eyes are better than one.

"Let us welcome the fact," I was saying with studied eloquence, "that it is not to a life of ignoble ease that the world of today is calling us; that the strife and controversy we now find ourselves surrounded by asks of us that we—"

It was just as I spoke of strife and controversy that I spotted the assassin and my assistant did the same. He did not need my signal but had already moved in.

The assassin was blocked so neatly and led off the field so quietly, that I doubt if even the president noticed. I finished my speech with coolness and aplomb, and I had the satisfaction of knowing that the president marveled at my self-possession in the face of danger. It was only afterward that he was told that the danger had been taken care of.

But meanwhile I had to sit there and endure the interminable handing out of degrees that followed. It was all very dull—very—

Griswold's glass was empty by then so we had no compunction in shaking him awake.

"How did you see the rifleman?" I demanded irritably. "Where was he? How did he smuggle the rifle onto the field and what gave him away?"

Griswold seemed to gather his wits with difficulty. Then he said, "*What* rifle? I told you over and over that a rifle was out of the question. I expected no rifle. The would-be assassin in his letter spoke of getting me 'in his sights' and of 'getting off a clear shot.' The English language is such that this could refer to a camera as well as a rifle and there are a thousand cameras at every commencement. Anyone could carry a camera onto the field. So I kept watching the people in front of me. When someone lifted a camera in my direction—someone who had taken no pictures at all earlier—my man saw him at once and nabbed him."

Jennings said, "You mean he just intended to take a picture of you?"

"Not quite," said Griswold. "If he had had the chance to push the button, a poisoned dart would have shot from the camera. It would probably have missed me, but if not, it might have poisoned me. The man was held for observation and is still in a mental hospital, I believe."

Irresistible to Women

Baranov sighed. "I wouldn't want to imply that I have not been adequately successful in my relationship with the fair sex, but I must admit that there is usually an exertion of charm required. It's becoming almost more trouble than it's worth."

The august confines of the Union Club were not often the sounding board of amatory reminiscences, I imagine, and I wasn't sure I wanted Baranov's. I said, "It needn't be trouble. With some people, the exertion of charm is second nature." I preened a little.

Jennings, however, said in a very snide way, "I've seen you at work and watched the women scatter. I'd try something else, if I were you."

And from the depths of the armchair, from which I could have sworn there had come the faint suspiration of placid snoring, Griswold's voice sounded. "I knew a man once who was irresistible to women. No question of charm at all. Just by existing, he found them gathering about."

"Lucky devil," said Baranov.

"It depends on your definition of luck," said Griswold. "One of the women in question killed him—"

I won't mention his name [said Griswold] or the names of the women involved. The incident made a medium-sized splash several decades ago, but it is now forgotten and might as well remain so. No need to revive the unpleasant past for survivors and descendants.

I was called in on the case by the police, by the

commissioner, in fact, who was a close friend of mine and who knew my facility for seeing to the heart of a matter, where lesser men would fail.

"Griswold," he said, "there are four women involved and any one of them could have been the murderess. Every one of them had the motive, means and opportunity, and it's just a matter of picking out the one among them who did it."

"The police can do that, can't they, if they dig around sufficiently? They have so limited a number of suspects."

The commissioner said, "Yes, but it will take time and manpower, something it will be difficult to spare at the moment. If you will simply interview each of the women, I'm sure you will be able to spot the guilty party at once."

I was always glad to help out the police, so I agreed to devote a day to it—something not lightly to be granted for I was a busy man in those days.

I can differentiate the four women for you easily, for one had black hair, one brown, one red, and one blond. They were apparently not the only women in his life, but they were the four who had each visited him in the course of the afternoon and early evening of the fatal day. Each of them had been more or less firmly put to one side and dismissed, for Irresistible had found a new woman and was, temporarily at least, abandoning the competition. Naturally, each of the four was considerably upset.

One of the four was sufficiently disturbed to return in the late evening in order to reason or plead with him. Apparently, she had found him adamant in his refusal, so she snatched up a kitchen knife, which was lying about the apartment, and sheathed it very neatly in his chest. She retained sufficient presence of mind to wipe the handle, then left. That, at least, was the reconstruction of the crime.

Fingerprints meant nothing elsewhere in the apartment: all four had been there. There were witnesses to the fact that a woman had returned in the late evening, but the particular woman simply could not be identified. It was dark, and there had been merely a casual glimpse.

None of the four had an adequate alibi for the period in question. All were upset and enraged over their dismissal, and any of the four could have snatched up the knife. The fifth woman, the new one in his life, came forward at once. She had no motive and she *did* have an alibi. She was simply not a suspect.

I interviewed all four women and found each to be astonished at the existence of the other three and that astonishment could not have been faked to a skilled investigator such as myself. I couldn't help feeling a great respect for Irresistible's ability to keep each one of his many women believing she was the only one.

Black-hair was firm on the irresistibility of the murdered man. "There was something about him," she said.

"Exactly what?" I asked.

"I'm not sure I can say."

"Extremely good-looking?" (I knew he wasn't. I had seen photographs.)

"No. Quite ordinary."

"Beautiful voice?"

"Not particularly."

"Educated? Cultured? Witty?"

"Who cares about that?"

"Good in bed?"

"Reasonably. I was attracted before I got to that."

"But you don't know exactly what it was that made him attractive."

"I can't say."

All four agreed on that. No one could put her finger on what it was that made him irresistible, but they all agreed he was.

I asked Red-hair if he used some particularly fetching aftershave lotion.

She said, "He didn't use any scent at all. Scentless soap. Scentless deodorant. That's something I liked about him, because I can't abide strong perfumes, either on my men or on myself."

That was one thing the four women had in common. They did not tend to choke you under a heavy pall of fragrant chemicals.

Brown-hair was the only one who showed sorrow.

She kept sniffing and her eyes were red. She said she didn't think any of them could have done it.

"Weren't you annoyed at his callous behavior?" I asked.

"Oh, yes, but only when I was away from him. Out of his presence, I could get pretty angry and furious." She blew her nose. "But when I was with him, that all melted away. All I knew was that I wanted him and wanted to be with him. There was just something about him. I'm sure the others felt the same way."

Just something about him. That was all I could get out of any of them.

Blond-hair seemed the most rattle-pated, the most willing to talk.

"How did you meet the man?" I said.

She said, "It was at a party. No one introduced us. I saw him off in the corner and I paid no attention. He was perfectly ordinary-looking and he didn't exactly catch my eye. But then I passed him and I couldn't help but notice something attractive about him. I just stopped and said, 'Hello.' He looked up and smiled and said, 'How are you?' and that's how we met."

"Something about the smile?" I asked. "A certain roguish charm?"

"N-no," she said. "Ordinary smile. We talked for a while. I don't remember about what."

"But you remember it was a fascinating conversation? Brilliant even?"

"N-no. I don't remember it at all. It must have been just ordinary. Still, he took me to his apartment and it was just wonderful being with him."

"Skillful at sex?"

"Not bad. I've had better. But it was just wonderful being with him."

She agreed with Brown-hair that in the actual presence of Irresistible she would not have been able to hurt him no matter what he did. All four agreed on that.

There was the possibility that the women were right. Perhaps not one of them had done it; perhaps it had been a male burglar. Presumably Irresistible did not exert his fascination on males.

A telephone call to the commissioner quashed that. No signs of forcible entry existed and nothing had been taken. Besides, the person seen coming to his apartment late at night had been a woman. Two witnesses agreed on that very firmly.

What was the nature of Irresistible's fascination? Somehow I felt that if I could but discover that, I would be able to solve the mystery.

I won't deny that I even played with the thought of magic.

Did Irresistible have some magic charm that turned the trick? Did he cast a spell on his victims, not in the figurative sense, but in the literal one?

I doubted that. After all, one of his victims had turned on him and killed him. If he were using a spell of some sort, surely he was sufficiently skillful not to have it fail him at a crucial moment. No, there had to be some *natural* ability he had, and *it* had failed him at the crucial moment. What had the ability been and how had it failed?

I made one more round of the women by telephone. I asked, "Did you ever speak to him on the telephone?"

They had.

"Did the conversation give you a warm feeling of love?"

Each one of them thought hard, then decided the telephone conversations were not particularly important.

"Did you like being held by him?"

Ecstatically.

"Even in the dark?"

Red-hair said emphatically, "It was better in the dark. I could concentrate on him more."

The others agreed.

Finally, I decided I had all I needed. I managed to get the answer to the commissioner before midnight. It had taken me one working day and I was right, of course—

Jennings was closest to Griswold and managed to tramp on his foot. "Don't go to sleep," he said. "What was the secret of his fascination?"

"Ouch," said Griswold, puffing out his white mustache and glaring. "Surely you can't be puzzled. If you're not going to call in the supernatural and talk of spells and love philters, then it's a matter of the senses. There are only three long-distance senses: sight, hearing and smell. It's clear that Irresistible was ordinary-looking and ordinary-sounding. Any one of the women could look at him from a distance or speak to him on the phone and be unaffected. It required a closer approach and that meant smell."

I said, "He didn't use scent. You said so."

"Exactly. But there are natural scents. The odor of clean perspiration can be aphrodisiac. Compounds have been located in traces from clean male perspiration that females find attractive. They have the odor of sandalwood, I believe. Undoubtedly, much of the attraction between the sexes is the result of these subtle chemical messages, but in our society, with its emphasis on heavy artificial scents and perfumes of all kinds, the natural scents are buried. Irresistible did not use such scents and perfumes. His natural odor was, I imagine, pronounced, and those women who likewise did not use scents and perfumes, and whose sense of smell was therefore sensitive, found him attractive. And they did so, in our smell-insensitive age, without even knowing why. That had to be it."

Baranov said, "Yes, but then who killed him?"

"That was self-evident. I told you that Brown-hair was the only one showing sorrow. She was sniffing and had red eyes. That may have been sorrow, but these things are also the symptoms of a cold in the nose. Undoubtedly, she could not have borne to hurt him, as she said; but with a cold, her sense of smell was temporarily gone. Temporarily, she was immune to Irresistible. Temporarily, there was nothing to stop her from knifing him—and she did."

He Wasn't There

The mood at the Union Club was one of isolation that night as the four of us sat in the library. It was fairly late and we had it to ourselves.

Jennings must have felt that sense of removal from the rest of the world, for he said dreamily, "If we just stayed here, I wonder if anyone would ever come looking for us."

"Our wives would miss us after a week or two," I said encouragingly. "The dragnet would be thrown out."

"Listen," said Baranov. "You can't rely on dragnets. Back in 1930, a certain Judge Crater stepped out onto the streets of New York and was never seen again. In fifty years, not a clue."

"Nowadays," I said, "with social security numbers, credit cards and computers, it's not that easy to disappear."

"Yes?" said Baranov. "How about James Hoffa?"

"I mean, deliberately," I said. "While still alive."

From the depth of his armchair, Griswold stirred and rumbled slowly to life. "In some way," he said, "it's easier to disappear now, I suppose. With today's increasingly heterogeneous society, its increasingly self-centered people, who's to care if one person, more or less, slips quietly through the mechanical motions of minimal social involvement? I knew a man once the Department was aching to find who simply wasn't there."

Jennings said quickly, "What Department?" but Griswold never answers questions like that.

*　　　*　　　*

I wonder [said Griswold] if you ever give thought to the careful putting together of small bricks of evidence into a careful edifice that isolates the foreign agent and neutralizes him. He doesn't have to be taken into custody and shot at sunrise. We have to know who and where he or she is. After that, he is no longer a danger. In fact, he becomes a positive help to us, particularly if the agent doesn't know he is known, for then we can see to it that he gets false information. He becomes *our* conduit and not theirs.

But it's not easy; or, at least, not always easy. There was one foreign agent who flickered always just beyond our focus of vision. Some of us called him Out-of-Focus.

And yet, little by little, we narrowed the search until we were convinced his center of operations was in a particular run-down building. We had his office located, in other words.

With infinite caution, we tried to track him down further without startling him into a change of base, which would mean having to redo all the weary work. We found threads of his existence at the local food stores, for instance, at the newsstands, at the post office, but we could never get a clear description or positive evidence that he was our man.

He remained Out-of-Focus.

We located the name he was using. It was William Smith and that gave us an idea.

Suppose a lawyer were looking for a William Smith who was a legatee for a sizable sum of money. In that case, neighbors would be delighted to help. If someone you know is likely to get a windfall, you *want* to help if only because that might induce gratitude and bring about the possibility of a loan. Smith himself might instinctively stand still for one moment if the possibility of money dangled before him, and even though he would know he was not the legatee, he might not question the search.

A real lawyer, amply briefed by ourselves, moved in to face William Smith—and he wasn't there. He hadn't been seen for days and no one had any information.

Only the superintendent of the small building seemed curious. After all, there was the question of the next month's rent, one might suppose.

The disappearance, though frustrating—he always seemed one step ahead of us—at least gave us a chance to institute a legitimate police search. Nothing dramatic: just a missing person's case. A local detective, rather bored, asked to see the apartment. The super let him in.

Two rooms, a kitchenette, a toilet. That was it. And it told us nothing useful about the occupant, except that he might have been a writer—and the super told us that much.

The days passed and no trace of William Smith could be picked up. He was no longer merely Out-of-Focus, he was clean gone, and we all had the rotten feeling he would be forever gone, like Judge Crater, and that he would be more dangerous than ever until we managed to get on the track again.

Then the boss did what he should have done in the first place.

He sent me to look about the apartment.

I was always good at presenting a rather bumbling appearance, even in my younger days. A useful thing, too, because it sets people off their guard. I was sure the super would talk the more freely for feeling sorry for me when I looked about the apartment helplessly.

He made no move to leave after he let me in, and of course I did not ask him to leave. He said, "Still looking for him, huh?"

"Yeah," I said. "I've got to fill out a report."

"His family must be plenty worried. You know he got a legacy or something, and I guess they want the money even if they don't want him."

I said, "I suppose," and kept on looking around.

One room was a library, not a big one, either the room or the library. The books were mostly reference and science books, so I suppose Smith could be considered a science writer—he had to have some cover. They weren't brand-new; some of them looked used. There was also one upholstered couch, one wooden rocking chair, and one end table in the room. That was all except for the bookcases.

The other room also had several bookcases, including one that contained an Encyclopaedia Britannica. It had a large desk, an upholstered armchair, several filing cabinets, an electric typewriter on a typewriting stand with a small swivel chair in front of it, a globe, and the minor paraphernalia of the writer's trade, such as reams of paper; also pens, paper clips, carbon paper, paperweights, envelopes, stamps and so on.

He was a very neat fellow. Everything was in the bookcases or in the filing cabinets or in the desk drawers or on top of the desk. Except for the items of furniture I've mentioned, there was nothing on the floor. Nor were there photographs of any kind and the walls were bare of anything framed.

There had been no useful fingerprints.

I said to the super, "You didn't take anything out, did you?" After all, he had a key.

"Who, me? With the police around? You crazy?"

I said, "You sure you can't describe the guy?"

"You guys asked me a million times. I tried, but he ain't much to look at. You know—just like a million other people."

I grunted. A successful agent has to look like a million other people or he's useless. They had taken the super to the local police station and had him look at endless pictures to locate someone who looked *like* William Smith and he ended by picking six pictures, and not one of the six looked anything like the other five. Smith remained Out-of-Focus.

There were two closets in the workroom. Clothes, of course. Nothing unusual.

I wandered into the bathroom. The usual toiletries, more or less used.

In the kitchenette, a sparse collection of comestibles in jars and cans. Some cutlery and pans and a can opener. None of it looked very used.

The super shrugged and said, "I suppose he ate out mostly. That's what I told the other guys."

"But you don't know where?"

He shrugged again, "I mind my own business. In this neighborhood, you got to."

"The guys at the station say you claim you talked to him sometimes."

"Well, you know, like when I come to collect the rent, or fix the shower when it leaks. Like that."

"What kind of stuff does he write."

"I don't know. Nothing *I* read, I can tell you that." He sniggered.

I said, "I don't see any books around with his name on them."

He said, "He said once he wrote for the magazines a lot. Maybe he don't write books. I don't think he used his own name, either. I think he said that once."

"What magazines did he write for?"

"I don't know."

"What name did he use?"

"I don't know that either. He never told me and I didn't ask. No business of mine."

"His typing ever bother the neighbors?"

"Nobody ain't never complained. Listen, in this house you could beat up on your old lady at three in the morning and set her to screaming like a banshee, and no one would complain."

"Did *you* ever hear the typing?"

"You mean in my apartment? Nah. I'm two floors down."

"I mean, in the hall?"

"Sure. Once in a while. Very light. An old building like this got good walls."

"Ever see him type?"

"Sure. I'd come to fix something and I'd hear the typewriter going, tap, tap. Like I said, lightly. He'd let me in and then he'd sit down again, and go back to typing. Probably didn't make much money out of it or he wouldn't live here." He sniggercd again.

I grunted and left. There were three other neighbors on the floor. None could describe the missing man; all insisted they knew nothing about him. One thought she could hear the typing sometimes, but she never paid any attention. "We keep ourselves *to* ourselves, mister," she said.

They surely did. There was no use pursuing the case any further.

For one thing, we didn't have to. Smith was now clearly in focus. Without his knowing it, we knew where he was and who he was and from that point on Smith was useless to the opposition and very useful to us— until such time as the opposition realized his cover had been broken. At that time we took him neatly into custody before they could arrange a fatal accident for him.

But if you don't mind, I'll go freshen my drink.

Griswold made as though to rise, but Jennings pulled his own chair in front of Griswold's and said, "You'll simply have to die of thirst unless you tell us first where and who he was."

Griswold drew his white eyebrows together in an annoyed frown. "You mean it isn't obvious? —There was *no* William Smith. He was a decoy designed to deflect the Department's attention if they ever got too close, and it almost worked. Thanks to one forgotten detail, however, it was clear to me that no one ever used that apartment for writing of any kind, and since the super claimed he had actually seen Smith typing, the conclusion was that it was the super himself who was maintaining the deception and that he was our man. That's all. Simplicity itself."

"No, it isn't," said Baranov. "How could you tell the apartment was never used for writing?"

"It lacked the essential. You can write without a library and without reference books. You can write without a desk. You can write without a typewriter. You don't even have to have ordinary paper. You can write on the back of envelopes or on shopping bags or in the margins of newspapers.

"But, gentlemen, any writer will tell you that there is one object that no writer can possibly do without, and that object was not in the apartment. I told you everything that was in the apartment and I didn't mention that object."

"But what was it?" I demanded.

Griswold's white mustache bristled. "A wastepaper basket! How can a professional writer do without that?"

The Thin Line

Griswold had been absent from the Union Club for several of our postprandial sessions, but now he sat there, to all appearances sound asleep. His shaggy white mustache puffed outward regularly under the force of his exhalations.

I said, "He can't have been away on business. He *must* be retired."

"Retired from what?" said Baranov skeptically. "You don't believe all those fairy tales he tells us, do you?"

"I don't know," said Jennings. "Most of them seem quite plausible."

"That's a matter of opinion," said Baranov. "For one thing, all those tales of spy and counterspy—I'll bet he gets them out of his imagination. Look here, I'm sure he's never left the country. What kind of a spy would never leave the country? What's there to do in the United States?"

Griswold's glass of scotch and soda, quite full, suspended midway even as he slept and (as ever) in no danger of spilling, moved slightly, as though operated by remote control, in the direction of his lips. It moved further and finally reached those lips. Griswold, with no sign of having awakened, sipped delicately, removed the glass and said, "I don't admit I have never left the country."

His eyes opened and he said, "And if I had never done so, there would still be plenty to occupy an agent right here at home. There is an honorable list of those who died right here under the Stars and Stripes—like Archie Davidson, to name just one.''

Archie Davidson [said Griswold] never left the United States, something which you uninformeds seem to think is true of me. Throughout his dozen years of service for the Department, however, Archie was never without something to do.

Does it occur to you gentlemen that there are well over a hundred foreign embassies and an even larger number of consulates in the United States?

Every single one of them must gather information that is of service to their nation, as our embassies and consulates do abroad in the service of our nation. Information gathering must be carried out more or less clandestinely and, in the case of a number of embassies, illegally, and for purposes that menace the security of our country.

Furthermore, the internal political battles of various nations are fought out on the territory of the United States. Various terrorist groups, or dissidents, or freedom fighters (they're called different things, according to viewpoint) operate here.

All these things must engage our attention and Archie was an excellent worker: unobtrusive, skilled and persuasive.

That he be persuasive was important, for one of the tasks of any skilled agent is that he manage to gain the confidence of someone on the other side. Someone working for the enemy is clearly a particularly reliable source of information, whether he is a defector on principle, a greedy fellow in search of money or other rewards, or simply an overconfident blabbermouth. Naturally, a defector on principle is the most reliable source and the one most likely to take large risks.

There was no one like Archie for finding the enemy who would work with us out of conviction and, at the time under discussion, he had one. We knew none of the details, of course, but the Department was pretty sure he had one. It was the easiest way of accounting for the nature and reliability of the information he fed us.

Nor did we try to find out what his source was. It makes sense not to do so.

When one has a spy in the enemy camp, the fewer who know his identity, the safer the spy and the connection. Even if the agent were to communicate the identity to a thoroughly reliable co-worker, the communication itself would be a point of weakness. Messages can be intercepted and interpreted, words overheard, gestures understood. The behavior of two people can serve as a more reliable lead for enemy eyes, than the behavior of one, the behavior of three still more so, and so on.

It is best, then, if there is a thin line between agent and enemy informer, a *very* thin line. If only the agent knows the informer, that is best. The informer himself feels more secure if he is confident that only one person knows what he is doing. He will then speak more freely. Archie had the ability to inspire that kind of confidence and he could do so because he had the conscious knowledge that he never double-crossed.

It was a very special loss to us when Archie was killed.

There was no way of telling that he had been killed in the line of duty. No one left a calling card. He was merely found dead in a doorway in a dubious street of one of our large eastern cities.

He had been knifed, and the knife had been withdrawn and was gone. His wallet was also gone, and it might be taken for granted that it was an ordinary mugging.

That is what the local police took it for, at any rate. Archie was not a well-known person; he had a professional unobtrusiveness and his cover was that of a clerk in a liquor store, so there was no reason for the police to give it special attention or for the press to stir much.

Nor could the Department take a very active interest. In the first place, we didn't find out about it till well after the fact. In the second, it would have been counterproductive to adopt too high a profile in the matter.

The killing *might* conceivably have been an ordinary

mugging with no connection whatever to Archie's work. In that case, it would certainly be a bad move to allow anyone watching the Department (and of course we are under surveillance by dozens of groups of undesirables) to learn, definitely, that Archie was an agent. That could lead them to other agents and could endanger much of our work. In particular, it might endanger the enemy informer that Archie was using and that we might perhaps salvage.

Then, too, we didn't really care whether Archie was killed by an ordinary mugger or by the enemy. We don't deal in revenge at the Department. We're not going to waste our time finding out who killed one of our men so that we can kill in return. Our work is more important than melodrama of that sort. Besides, even if Archie were killed, let us say, at the orders of an important foreign embassy, the actual murderer might well be a hired hophead, who wouldn't even remember the details of the hiring.

No, what was important to us was Archie's work, not Archie. And the most important part of his work at the time he was killed was his link to the enemy informer— that thin line that was so thin it stretched between two people only, and that was snapped when one of those two people was killed.

Unless, of course, Archie had somehow managed to give information that could allow us to reconstruct the thin line. It didn't seem likely that he could have done so, but it would have been his duty to do so if he could and this therefore had to be followed up.

Naturally, I was the one sent to deal with the police. My air of calm authority always worked well with them and smoothed the troubled waters that inevitably arose when the local law-enforcement people thought they were going to be overwhelmed by the Feds.

I spent considerable time in indirection that served to obscure the exact reason why Washington might be interested, but I won't bother you with that. I will tell it far more directly than it actually was.

I said, "Was he still alive when he was found?"

"Hell no. He'd been dead at least three hours."

"Too bad. It's always nice when there's still life in them and they can say something."

"You mean like 'The man who killed me was—' and then they croak before they can get the word out?"

"We like them to get the word out. He didn't leave any messages, I suppose?"

"You mean, written in his own blood on the sidewalk?" The homicide man seemed to be trying to get a rise out of me, but I didn't oblige. He said, "There was some blood soaked into the jacket he was wearing, but none near or on his hands. What's more, there was nothing scrabbled in the dust; no words formed out of banana peels and other garbage. Listen, his wallet was gone and it was all we could do to work out his identity."

"His pockets were searched?"

"Of course."

"Anything interesting? Do you have a list?"

"I have better than that," said the detective. "Here's the stuff itself." He upended a plastic bag and let it all spill out on his desk.

I went over the material. Keys, change, a small pocket comb, a memo book, an eyeglass case, a ball-point pen. I looked through the memo book. There was nothing in it, though several of the leaves were torn out. A good agent puts as little on paper as possible. If for some reason he must record something, he gets rid of it as soon as possible.

"Anything else?" I asked.

The detective shook the plastic bag wordlessly. A little wad of paper fell out to his apparent surprise. I picked it up and spread it out. It said in straggly capital letters: CALL TAXICAB.

The paper was from the memo book. I used the ball-point to make marks on a piece of scrap paper on the desk. It was the right color and thickness.

I said, "Was this written after he was stabbed?"

The detective shrugged. "Could be."

"Which pocket was this found in? Was it found wadded? Where was the pen?"

We had to locate the officer who had first found Archie and the detective who had then arrived on the scene. The results seemed conclusive. The paper, wadded, was in the left jacket pocket; the fountain-pen with Archie's right hand holding it in the right jacket pocket. If no one had considered all this, it was because no importance was attached to the murder.

It was clear, however, that Archie's last effort, like the good agent he was, gave us important information. It had to be some reference to his contact, some way of reconstituting the thin line.

I considered. Archie didn't say which taxicab to call. Was it a particular company? Did he use a particular company and could we find out which it was? Was there some message we could gather if we used the Yellow Pages and turned to the "taxicab" entry? Or was it something else?

I thought very intensively for a minute or so and then took a course of action that located the enemy informer and reconstituted the link. Before the other side located the informer and dealt with him, we had had time to gather some important items of information that helped in the satisfactory resolution of the Cuban missile crisis. So it was a happy ending—

"No you don't," I said, tramping hard on his shoe to keep him awake. "You haven't told us the important thing."

Griswold frowned. "Certainly, I did. I took a course of action that located the enemy informer and—"

"Yes, but *how?* What taxicab company did you call?"

"I didn't call any. Good God, man, don't tell me you don't understand. When you make a local phone call, you dial seven numbers. Each number, from 2 to 9, has three letters associated with it, dating back to the days when exchanges had names. We have ABC in the 2 position, DEF in the 3 position and so on. It's possible to give a telephone number in terms of letters if there are no 1's or 0's in it. There are no letters at all associated with 1; and only a Z associated with 0 on *some* dials.

"So I didn't call any taxicab company. I dialed T-A-X-I-C-A-B, which in numbers is 829-4222. That was the contact point. Undoubtedly, Archie found it easier to remember the word than the number combination and when dying, the word was all he remembered—so he scrawled it in desperation.''

Mystery Tune

Baranov rustled his paper with definite annoyance as we sat within the august confines of the Union Club that evening. He said, "There's been another gang killing in Brooklyn."

"What else is new?" I asked, unimpressed.

"Well, damn it," said Baranov, "now they'll put in who knows how many police man-hours on the case while valuable police work languishes. Who cares if one gangster kills another? Let them."

"It sets a bad precedent," said Jennings sententiously. "Murder is murder and you can't let it go. Besides, you don't really know it's a gang killing till you investigate."

"Then again," I added, "hardly any of them are ever solved, so maybe the police don't waste too much time."

"Yes, they do," responded Baranov hotly. "There's plenty of waste, however little time they spend on it. No one involved will talk and the police aren't allowed to beat it out of them. Even close relatives of the victim won't talk, the damn fools. You'd think they'd want to see the murderer caught."

It was at this time that Griswold stirred. His soft snore ended in a brief period of near strangulation and, recovering, he smoothed his white mustache with the hand that wasn't holding his scotch and soda.

He said, "Of course they want to see the murderer get his, but not by police procedure. They want it by gang vengeance, which is more sure in any case. The criminal ethic depends on the closed mouth. Without that, the forces of society learn too much and they all suffer. There was the case once—"

For a moment, it looked as though he might drop off again, but Jennings, who was seated closest, kicked his ankle and Griswold's eyes opened wide. With a soft "ouch" he continued—

There was the case once [said Griswold] of Eighty-eight Jinks. He was christened Christopher, I believe, but he was a pianist by talent and the way he stroked the eighty-eight keys rechristened him. At least, no one ever called him anything else but Eighty-eight to my knowledge.

He might have become a great pianist, too, many people thought. He could play anything he had ever heard, in any style, and could improvise chords that would tear your heart out. He had a good voice, too. Something was missing, though. The drive wasn't there. And he drank quite expertly and that ruined what chance remained.

By the time he was thirty-five, he was making a precarious living by tinkling the keys in various barrooms and second-rate night spots, and running errands for the gangs. He was a gentle guy even when he was the worse for drink—which was most of the time, though that never seemed to get in the way of his fingers on the keyboard.

The police knew him well and laid off him generally. He never made a nuisance of himself, so there was never occasion to lodge a drunk-and-disorderly charge against him. He did not use drugs or push them; he had no part in the operations of the ladies of the evening, who infested the establishments for which he played; and the errands he ran for the boys were innocuous enough as such things go.

Sometimes the police did try to pump him for something, but he would never talk.

One time he said, "Look, fellows, it don't do me any good to be seen with you. It ain't just me. I got a sister who works hard, and she's married and got a little kid. I ain't no credit to her and just my being alive does her enough harm. I don't want to bring her anything worse.

I don't want her hassled and she'll *be* hassled if anyone thinks I'm with the cops too much."

And that, of course, is one reason why people are so closemouthed even when you would think that it would be to their interest to talk. It never is. Talking is the unforgivable sin and the strikeback is not only at the talker, but at those near to him.

So the police let him alone, because they saw his point and knew he wouldn't talk and that he didn't have anything to talk about anyway.

Which made it sad when he was knocked off.

He was found with a knife in his back in an alley. When the police got there he was still alive, because for once the knifing was reported. At least someone called in to say there were cries of help from the alley. Whoever called didn't leave his name, of course, and hung up quickly, but we don't usually get even that much in that neighborhood. Generally, the corpse is found only well after the fact, after which everyone in the neighborhood gets glassy-eyed when questions are asked and a surprising number of them turn out not even to speak English.

The police never found out why Eighty-eight was knifed. Anyone would have thought he was harmless enough. On the other hand, there are internal politics in gangs, as anywhere else, and some errand that Eighty-eight had run might well have discomfited a gang member in some way.

The policeman who was on the scene knew Eighty-eight well, and once he found the poor fellow alive, sent out the call for an ambulance at once. Eighty-eight stared at the policeman peacefully, with no look of concern in his eyes.

The policeman said, "We'll get you out of here, Eighty-eight. You'll be all right."

Eighty-eight smiled. "What are you talking about, cop? I'm dying. I'll be all right? When I die, I'll be all right. I'll be down in hell with my friends and my hopes, and if they've got a redhot piano down there, I'll manage."

"Who did this to you, Eighty-eight?"

"What's it to you, or to anyone?"

"Don't you want to get the rat who did this to you?"

"Why? If you get him, does that mean I heal up? I die anyway. Maybe he did me a favor. If I had guts I'd of done this to me myself years ago."

"We've got to get him, Eighty-eight. Help us out. If you're dying, it won't hurt you. What can he do to you? Dance on your grave?"

Eighty-eight smiled more weakly. "Probably won't find no grave. I'll just be dumped on the garbage heap—with the other garbage. They won't dance there; they'll dance on my sister. Can't have that. I'd appreciate it if you'd just let it be known I didn't say *nothing*."

"We'll say that, Eighty-eight, don't worry. But make it a lie. Just give us a name, or a hint, or a sign with your head. Anything. Look, Eighty-eight, it could help me out on my job and I won't let on you did anything."

Eighty-eight seemed faintly amused. "You want help? All right, how's this?" His fingers moved as though they were tapping on invisible piano keys and he hummed a few notes of music.

"What's that?" asked the policeman.

"Your hint, cop. I can't talk no more."

Eighty-eight closed his eyes and died en route to the hospital.

They called me in the next day. It was getting to be a habit with them and I didn't like it. I had work of my own to do and helping them brought me thanks, but nothing tangible. I couldn't even get a traffic ticket fixed out of it.

I said, "A gangland killing? Who cares? What's the difference if you solve it or not?" The natural reaction, in other words.

I was talking to Carmody, a lieutenant in the homicide division.

He said, with a growl, "Do I have to get that from you? Isn't it enough we get it from idiots in general. For one thing, the guy who got it was a poor bastard who harmed no one but himself and who deserved better of life—but let's not be sentimental. Look at it this way—

"If we can pin this on someone, we shake up the organization he belongs to. That might amount to nothing. We might not get a conviction, or, if we do, the gang carries on without him. But there's a chance—just a chance—that the shake-up will work cracks in the organization. We might be able to take advantage of those cracks and bust it wide open and pick up the pieces as far as Newark. We've got to play for that, Griswold, and you've got to try to help us."

"But how?" I asked.

"We've got a lead to the killer. I want you to talk to Officer Rodney, who was with Eighty-eight Jinks—he's the dead man—before he died."

Officer Rodney did not look happy. Having a lead he could neither understand nor communicate was no road to advancement.

Painstakingly, he told us of the conversation with Eighty-eight, the same conversation I myself have just described. I don't know how accurate his account was, but, of course, it was the tune that counted.

I said to him, "What kind of tune?"

"I don't know, sir. Just a few notes."

"Did you recognize it? Ever hear it before? Can you name it?"

"No, sir. I never heard it before. It didn't sound like it was part of a popular song or anything like that. Just a few notes that didn't sound like anything."

"Can you remember it? Can you hum it or sing it?"

Rodney looked at me rather horrified. "I'm not much of a singer."

"We're not holding auditions. Just do your best."

He tried several times and then gave up in complete misery. "I'm sorry, sir. He only sang it once and it was like nothing I ever heard. I can't come up with anything."

So we let him go, and he looked relieved at the chance of getting away from questioning that made him seem helpless.

Carmody looked at me anxiously. "What do we do? Do you suppose we could have him put under hypnosis? He might remember then."

I said, "Suppose we did, and he remembered the tune and we recogized it and saw the relationship to a suspect. Could we introduce it all as evidence? Would Rodney survive cross-examination? Would it be convincing to a jury?"

"No, to all three. But if we were satisfied we knew who it was, we could try to break him down—find motive, means and opportunity."

"Do you have any suspects at all?"

"There's a neighborhood gang, of course, and they include three men we have good reason to think have been involved in past killings."

"Get after all three, then."

"Not convincing. If you're after all three, none are scared, since we're clearly in the dark. And it might be someone else altogether, too. If we knew one man and zeroed in on him and him alone—"

"Well," I said, "what are the names of the three suspects you just mentioned."

He said, "Moose Matty, Ace Begad and Gent Diamond."

"In that case," I said, "we may not have a problem. Get Officer Rodney and get us both to the nearest piano."

We located a piano in the studio across the street and I said to Rodney, "Listen to this, officer, and tell me if this is what Eighty-eight hummed." I tapped out several notes.

Rodney looked surprised. "It does sound like it, sir! Could you do it again?"

I did it again. "Just this one more time, officer," I said, "or you'll start believing it to be the tune no matter what I play. Now is this it?"

"Yes it is," he said in excitement. "That's it exactly."

"Thank you, officer. Good job and I'm sure you'll get a commendation for it.—Lieutenant, we know who the murderer is, or at least we know who Eighty-eight said it was."

Well, I don't know whether there were repercussions as far as Newark, because I didn't follow the case thereafter, but I understand they got the murderer and even put him in prison, which is a happy ending. Officer Rodney got a commendation; Lieutenant Carmody got the credit; I got back to my own work; and all of you, of course, see what happened.

*　　*　　*

"No, we don't," roared Jennings, "and don't go to sleep on us. This time, Griswold, you have gone too far and you're simply putting us on. How could you reconstruct the notes and how could you use them to spot the murderer?"

Griswold snorted. "Where's the need for explanation? There are only seven notes and then the eighth starts the series over again—*do, re mi, fa, sol, la, ti,* and then *do* starts it over. Well, they are also expressed as letters: C, D, E, F, G, A, B, and then C again. You've heard of 'middle C' and the 'key of G' or 'D minor and so on.

"Very well. It is possible, though not usual, for a name to consist only of the note letters of A through G. Ace Begad is an example, and as soon as I heard it, I felt sure he was the murderer. I spelled the name in musical notes: *la, do, mi, ti, mi, sol, la, re* or A, C, E, B, E, G, A, D, with a short pause between the third and fourth notes and Rodney recognized the combination when I played it—and that's all there was to it."

Hide and Seek

"I see," said Baranov, peering slyly in the direction of Griswold, "where two agents have been convicted of searching a place without a warrant."

He paused and neither Jennings nor I said anything. Griswold was at right angles to us, facing the fireplace in which a log smoldered, for it was a rather chilly fall evening. For a wonder, he wasn't asleep, for his scotch and soda moved slowly to his lips and then away again. But he said nothing.

Baranov tried again. "This sort of thing makes it hard for law-enforcement agencies to do their work; especially if they must work in secrecy and in the interest of national security."

Another pause. Jennings said in a slightly higher voice, "On the other hand, you can't let law-enforcement agents break the law they are sworn to defend. That puts the liberties of the people in direct jeopardy."

At that point, Griswold swiveled his chair, faced the three of us with his eyebrows hunched over his china-blue eyes and his white mustache twitching. He said, "You're trying to get a reaction out of me and you're wasting your time. It is not so much a question of law as of prudence. They could have done what they did with impunity, if they had been given a direct mandate by those who were entitled to judge when something was a matter of national security. They did not obtain the proper authority, and not merely a search warrant. Let me tell you. What can hold back an organization far

more than just legal constraints is its own set of mind—
which can be foolish. For instance—"

He took another delicate sip at his scotch and soda
and then went on.

For instance [said Griswold] back in the days when
the agency was run by you-know-who, there wasn't an
agent who dared lift his voice against any ukase, however ridiculous. After all, senators threw themselves
over mud puddles so the chief could use them to avoid
getting his shoes muddy, and presidents cowered in the
corner when he frowned.

You could tell an agent a mile away by their chief-
imposed uniforms. No one else had shirts so white, so
glossy, so buttoned-down, or ties so narrow and so neatly
centered, or suits so subdued, or waistlines so carefully
flat, or hair so short and so neatly parted, or was scented
in so masculine a fashion, or seemed so much younger
and callower than his years. Well, they might just possibly have been mistaken for Mormon missionaries, but
for nothing else.

And of course, they were all in a state of constant
terror. It was not so much that they might make a
mistake. That might be forgiven. The real fear was that
they might make the agency, and the chief, look foolish.
For that it was evisceration the first time. There was no
forgiveness and the agents knew it.

Naturally, I could never make it with the agency in
any official capacity. I wouldn't shave my mustache,
which was dark in those days but almost as impressive
as it is now, and I wouldn't wear the uniform, and worst
of all, I once chose to look over the head of the chief,
which was easy to do, and to pretend I didn't see him.
He might forget anything else, but he never forgot a slur
on his height, however indirect.

It didn't matter. I made out. When things got tough
there was many an agency official who came to me for
help.

Jack Winslow came to me once, I remember, with an
ingratiating smile on his face and some telltale beads of
sweat on his forehead, despite the rule that no agent

must perspire. Jack Winslow was his real name, by the way, which helped him a lot at the agency. The only better name would have been Jack Armstrong.

He said, "Listen, Griswold, the damndest thing happened today and I'd appreciate it if you would let me have your thoughts on it."

"Tell me what happened," I said, "and I'll tell you if I have any thoughts about it. And I won't tell the chief you asked me."

He thanked me very sincerely for that, but, of course, there was no way I could tell the chief if I wanted to. We were not on speaking terms—which suited me fine.

There's no point in telling you Winslow's story in full detail because he's an awfully tedious fellow. Still is, I understand, though he's retired now. I'll give you the essentials in brief.

The agency had gotten on to the fringes of an operation it was important to stop. They had located a pawn in the game. They could pick him up any time they wanted to, but it would have done them no good. He wouldn't know enough and he could be too easily replaced. If he were left at large, however, he might be used as a wedge that could pry out something far more useful than himself. It was tedious and delicate work, and sometimes this sort of thing was fumbled and no agent was ever allowed to enjoy that fumble—so Winslow was in a difficult position.

The goal at this particular time was to spot a relay: the passage of something important from one person to another. Two items of information were desired: the manner of the surreptitious passage, because that could be an important clue to the system of thought being used by these people; and the identity of the pickup, that is, the one who received the item, for the pick-up was likely, but not certain, to be more important than the transmitter.

The pawn had been maneuvered into accepting something to put through the relay. It was something that was legitimately important; though not as important as the others had been led to believe. Still, they were not fools and had to be fed *something* in order to make them bite.

It was important enough, at any rate, to make the agents prefer not to lose it without having gained something at least equally important.

The real coup was the shape of the object to be transferred. Somehow the opposition had been persuaded to order their pawn to pick up a package which, while not heavy, was six feet long and about four inches wide. It looked like a packaged fishing rod and there was no way in which it could be disguised or made to look inconspicuous. Winslow was proud of this and wouldn't tell me how the trick had been turned, but I didn't care. I knew that, as a general rule, the people we fight against are as vulnerable as we are.

There were five agents at various places and in various forms watching the progress of the pawn or, rather, of the very conspicuous package. They didn't stay close; they couldn't have, or they would have been easily spotted by their white shirts and beautiful gray fedoras in a neighborhood in which neither was ever seen on the inhabitants.

The pawn walked into a crummy restaurant in this slummish neighborhood. He had to maneuver the package to get it through the door, and Winslow held his breath lest he break it, but he got it into the restaurant in one piece. He stayed there about five minutes—four minutes, twenty-three seconds, Winslow told me, since he had stupidly been watching his watch instead of the restaurant—and then he came out. He didn't have the package with him, or anything that could possibly have held it.

They expected that. Somehow, though, they expected that it would come out in the hands of someone else, or in *some* fashion, and it never did. After two hours, Winslow got very uneasy. Could they have frightened off the pick-up by being insufficiently clandestine in their surveillance? They couldn't help that as long as they wore their uniform, but that wouldn't protect them against the chief's wrath.

Worse yet, could they have allowed the package—six feet long, four inches wide—to be slipped out under their noses somehow? If so, their careers were finished.

Finally, Winslow could stand no more. In desperation, he ordered his men into the restaurant, and then came the final blow.

"It wasn't there," said Winslow desperately. "It wasn't such a damned big place and the package just wasn't there. As soon as I could see that was the situation, I came here. I remembered you lived only a mile away and hoped you might be in." He looked decidedly grateful I *was* in.

I said, "I suppose I can trust your agents to find it if it's there. Something six feet long isn't exactly a diamond or a piece of microfilm."

"It's not there."

"Could it have been dismembered, taken apart, hidden in parts, or, for that matter, taken out in parts?"

"No, it would then be broken, useless. It had to be intact.—I'm not telling you what it is, mind you."

"I'm not asking and you probably don't know yourself. —Did you look over the people in the restaurant?"

"Certainly. They were the type who were completely uncooperative, who turn sullen and resentful at the least sign of the law. But there's no way something like that could be hidden on anyone's person."

"By the way," I said, "do you have a search warrant?"

Winslow reddened a bit. "We have a sort of catchall search warrant for safety violations. Never mind about that."

I'm sure it wouldn't have held up in court, but in those days such things weren't questioned.

I said, "Maybe it was taken upstairs."

"There is no upstairs. It's a crummy little one-story greasy-spoon restaurant, between two tenements."

"Well then," I said, "there must be an entrance into one of the adjoining tenements, or both."

"Not a chance. Solid wall, both ways."

"Cellar?"

"We looked through it. A junkyard with some food staples. What we wanted wasn't there."

"Entrances into the adjoining tenements through the cellar?"

"No. Damn it, Griswold, give us some credit for brains."

"Kitchen?"

"Plenty of cockroaches; nothing of what we wanted."

"Egress from the kitchen?"

"There was a door to a back alley, where they put out the garbage—such garbage as they didn't serve—but we had a man there and I assure you he's reliable. People came out long enough to dump garbage and then went back in.—And before you ask, he looked through the garbage cans, something that didn't require much detail work, since an intact six-foot package would—"

"Stick out like a sore thumb. Rest rooms?"

"I looked through it carefully myself. Personally. Two stalls. I looked in both of them and both were empty, thank goodness. I even checked the urinals, so help me, just in case they were loose and you could slip a six-foot package into the wall behind them. There was a small window, caked with dust and old paint. No way of opening it and the glass was unbroken."

I said, "If the pawn took it in and didn't take it out, then it must still be in the restaurant."

"But it isn't. I swear."

"Then if it isn't there, it must have been sneaked out—a six-foot package with five agents watching."

Winslow winced. "That couldn't be."

"One or the other," I said.

But Winslow looked so miserable, I relented. I said, "Stop suffering, Winslow. I'll save your hide. I know where it is."

And it was where I knew it was. And I *did* save his hide.

Griswold just sat there smiling at us fatuously. Then he leaned back in his chair as though he were about to close his eyes.

I said, "Come on, Griswold. This time you've gone too far. You couldn't possibly know where it was. I defy you to explain yourself."

"Defy? Defy? Good God, man, it was so easy. I told you what agents were like and what their chief had trained them to be. They might dash fearlessly into enemy fire, they might fearlessly search a place quite illegally. But not one of the chief's men would think of doing anything that was downright unmannerly and crude. They would poke about everywhere but one place—a place they probably didn't even let themselves realize existed."

"What are you talking about?" said I.

"With regard to the rest rooms, Winslow said, 'I looked through *it* carefully myself.' *It*. Singular! It was the men's room, because it had urinals. He mentioned them. Well, a restaurant can't possibly have a men's room without having one for women, too. Our culture demands that symmetry. But what respectable agent would dream of walking into a ladies' room, even in a slum restaurant?"

"You mean the pawn hid it there?"

"Sure. I imagine he listened to make sure it was empty, then he opened it and propped it up against one corner. Any woman entering that crummy rest room would have neither leisure nor desire to investigate the package, or do anything but go in and get out. Even if the room were not empty, it could be done so quickly, the woman inside would have had no time to scream. In any case, that's where Winslow and his men found the package when they forced themselves to look."

"But why would he put it there?"

"As it turned out on another occasion, the pick-up was a woman. So why not?"

Gift

For the last two or three weeks, Griswold had remained grimly silent during our weekly get-togethers in the quiet library of the reclusive Union Club, a room that, by common consent, no one but the four of us used on those nights.

It was rather depressing, for we reluctantly agreed that the evening lost part of its charm without one of his tales, whether or not they were true—which was something none of us could ever decide.

I said, "Listen. I have something to say that can't fail to draw him out. Just follow my lead."

I turned to the old armchair that had long since fitted itself to the contours of Griswold's angular body and that no one else in the Club dared use even on the evenings he wasn't there, which weren't many.

I said, "I read in the papers that they have now, through use of computers, invented coding systems that are so complicated that breaking them, even with the use of another computer, is impossible."

Baranov said, "Well, there goes the entire profession of espionage."

"Good riddance," said Jennings emphatically.

Griswold's hand had trembled just slightly at my remark as it held the scotch and soda, though I knew there was no chance of his dropping it, even if he did seem fast asleep. With Baranov's remark, his feet shuffled a bit as though he were thinking of standing up and leaving. Finally, when Jennings made his observation, one eyelid went up and revealed Griswold's blue-ice eye glaring at us.

He said, "You can send all your codes to the devil. A clever person can send a message in the clear and have it perfectly mysterious—to anyone but the equally clever man who receives it."

"Like yourself, you mean," I said. "Which did you do? Send or receive?"

Griswold took a small sip at his drink and said, "Receive."

I suppose [said Griswold] that there isn't an espionage organization in the world that doesn't have its mole: someone working for the other side who has infiltrated the intelligence community. It's probably the world's hardest, most dangerous and most difficult profession, since a good mole must be prepared to spend years, perhaps decades, of his life, living a lie and working for his host country with complete dedication—except that it is his job to see to it that his own country gets the information it needs without the host country finding out where the leak is.

We have a number of good moles abroad and we certainly count on being plagued by moles ourselves. A good percentage of our effort consisted in moving heaven and earth to locate enemy moles and then moving earth and heaven to maintain the cover of our own moles.

Our best mole was Rudolf Schwemmer—which was his real name, by the way. All the people I will mention in this account are either dead or retired, so it will do no harm to use their names.

Rudolf Schwemmer was a German, of course. Not a German-American, but a German, and an Aryan German at that. He looked the precise image of the heroic young German of the Nazi posters, but he had been no Nazi. He had fought Hitler from the very beginning, had escaped to England in 1938 and then returned to Germany during the war to do what he could to unite and strengthen such elements of opposition as existed there.

He could speak English well enough, but with a distinct German accent, and he was truly at ease only with German. This meant we couldn't use him in the Soviet Union, but he was perfect for work within Germany.

For years after the war, he had been part of the East-German spy apparatus, working himself higher and higher in its ranks, and reporting always to us. And through East Germany, we always knew a good deal of what was going on in all the nations of the East European bloc, including the Soviet Union. His real identity was only known to a very few top men in our organization.

One thing we desperately wanted to know was the identity of the mole in our own ranks. That there was one, we were sure. The Soviets knew too much and, by a process of elimination, it was our own organization that supplied the leaks. And it had to be someone of high rank.

That was a terrible blow to those of us on top. When one of us didn't know which of the few others of high rank could be trusted, we all began to fall into a paranoid frenzy.

And Schwemmer came through.

At least he almost came through. We received messages in the usual fashion and by the usual route to the effect that he had the answer and that it was certain. He wouldn't give it, though, until the top men of the organization were all in one room and under guard, so that when the truth was revealed the legitimate members of the organization could place the mole under instant arrest.

So four of us gathered in the conference room, with three guards placed at each of the two exits. We had carefully identified ourselves to the guards, who then, under instructions, searched us for concealed weapons or suicide pills.

We sat around the mahogany table staring at each other somberly. I imagine that three of us were wondering which of the other three was going to be under arrest in the next few minutes, while the fourth, who was the mole, was wondering if he was really facing a long term of imprisonment at the very least. Naturally, he—the mole, I mean—could not have refused to attend, for that refusal would have given him away at once.

I was one of the four, of course. The others were all considerably older than I was, and my betters in rank and experience, but not in brilliance, you can be sure.

There was Judson Cowles at the table. He was acting chief of the organization and was then still waiting for Senate confirmation. The second in command was Seymour Norman Hyde, a determinedly friendly guy who always used first names, and who had been in the organization since it was first formed. There was the chief of the code division, who was Morris Q. Yeats. We never found out what the Q stood for, but it was always my guess that it was Quintus.

Yeats had arranged to have the message brought to us the instant it arrived. No one was to decode it but we ourselves.

The message arrived precisely on time and was delivered by one of the guards, who then stepped back to the other side of the door. The chief himself opened the envelope and removed the paper inside in such a way as to make sure we could all see it. It was a nasty shock when all we found on it was one word: "gift."

"What does that mean, Yeats?" said the chief abruptly.

"I don't know. Do you have any ideas, Hyde?"

Hyde shrugged his shoulders. "I'm as much in the dark as you, Morris. Why don't you call the Code Room? It could be that the message has been switched en route."

The chief looked disdainful at that suggestion, but he called. By the time we were through speaking, it was clear that the message was authentic. It was also clear what had happened.

Schwemmer, our man in East Germany, had sent the revelation just a few minutes too late. He had been uncovered and arrested. They must have been at the door even while he was preparing to send the message and, in the end, with the door breaking down behind him, he had time for only one word, and a short one at that. We were pretty sure that was the last word we'd ever get from him.

"It tells us nothing," said Yeats.

"It may be," said Hyde with a judicious pull at his pipe, "that the word is coded. Is that possible, Morris?"

Yeats, who hated having his first name used in the patronizing manner Hyde always managed to affect said with emphasis, "No—Sy! In the code that Schwemmer used, 'gift' can't be twisted into anything sensible—nor can it in any other code we use. He must have sent it in the clear; no time to send a prepared message."

"But it doesn't mean anything," said Hyde. He didn't mind in the least having Yéats use his nickname. If he had his pseudodemocratic way, everyone would. He went on, "Do you see anything there, chief?"

Cowles said, "No, I don't."

I said, "With all respect, chief, we'd better see *something*. We four were the only ones who knew Schwemmer's true identity. One of us must somehow have tipped off the East Germans."

"If one of us knew," said Cowles, "he would have blown Schwemmer's cover long ago. This could mean that all four of us are loyal."

I wouldn't let him get away with that. I wasn't popular with the other three; I was too young to be doing so much talking. But I had to do it, since no one else in the organization had the brains for it. I said, "Revealing Schwemmer's name to the enemy would have risked blowing his own cover. There are too few capable of doing that and he would quickly have been detected. He only did it now, whoever he is, in desperation, since he was about to be exposed in any case if he didn't. As it was, he waited irresolutely to the last minute, wondering if he ought rather to chance Schwemmer's being wrong. If he hadn't waited just a trifle too long, Schwemmer wouldn't have been able to send us even this one word."

"Which tells us nothing," said Cowles.

"It's got to tell us something," I said. "Schwemmer knew all four of us reasonably well. Each one of us has met him at one time or another. This word must apply to one of us."

Hyde said, "Maybe he intended a longer word, but was interrupted in the middle."

Yeats said, "There is no word that starts with g-i-f-t, but 'gift' itself. Look it up in the dictionary if you don't believe me."

Hyde said, "It could have been more words, not

necessarily a longer word. Suppose it was supposed to be 'gift horse in the mouth.' "

"What would that mean?" said Cowles, who was beginning to sweat visibly.

"I don't know" said Hyde "because that isn't the message. It could be anything. It's just that we'll never know."

I said impatiently, " 'Gift' may mean something."

"Like what?" said Yeats acidly. "Does it refer to you because you think you're God's gift to the organization?"

That was just his jealousy speaking, and I let it go by.

Hyde said, with a thin smile, "Well—Morris—suppose we remember that you were assigned to us from the Treasury Department three years ago and that you're still theoretically on temporary status. You're a gift to us from the Treasury Department."

Yeats said, "Go to hell—Sy. Just remember that the chief is up for confirmation in the Senate. If the Senate pleases, the chief will stay chief; if not, you may become chief, Sy. So the two of you, either one, could be viewed, so to speak, as the gift of the Senate."

"Ridiculous," said Cowles, reddening. "We can't play foolish games like this. If the message isn't a clear-cut indication, it is useless. It is clearly useless. We'll have to try again from scratch."

"Wait," I said. "The message is clear; it is obvious who our traitor is. If you will call in the guards, chief, I will name him and once he is in custody, I will explain how I know. If I'm wrong, he can be released and I, of course, will resign."

Naturally, I wasn't wrong.

I said, "Don't stop now, Griswold, or I knock that scotch and soda right out of your hand."

Griswold eyed me belligerently and, with great deliberation, finished his drink. He put the glass on the table and wiped his mustache and only then did he hunch his white eyebrows at me and say, "You don't see it, either? What idiots!"

He went on. "See here, I told you Schwemmer spoke English but that he was at ease only with German. In the final emergency of his life, with the door breaking down behind him, with the prospect of torture and execution about certain, he had no time to think in any language but German; and besides, the German word was shorter."

"What German word?" asked Baranov, puzzled.

" 'Gift' is an English word, but it is also a German word which means something altogether different. The German 'gift' means 'poison.' ' "

We remained puzzled. Jennings said, " 'Poison' makes no more sense than 'gift.' "

"It doesn't?" said Griswold. "With one of us named Seymour Norman Hyde, who likes to be called by his first name? What do you think Sy N. Hyde is, if not poison—and the most familiar poison of all, which has almost the same name, by the way, in English and German."

Hot or Cold

Jennings sighed heavily, and the sound seemed to produce an echo in the cavernous, dim and slightly dusty confines of the library of the Union Club. "I'm getting old," he said. "There's no use denying it anymore. I've just had a birthday and my kids are getting suspiciously kind to me. They did everything but tuck a shawl about my shoulders."

I said unsympathetically, "Do you have arthritis?"

"No, I don't."

"Then you're not old. Old age starts when you become creaky; when it hurts to sit down or stand up and when your joints ache even when you're not doing anything. Except for that, sixty feels like twenty if you're in reasonable shape." I said it all rather smugly. I don't have arthritis and I can do everything the twenty-year-olds can do.—That I want to do, I mean; I don't want to play football.

Baranov said, "It isn't arthritis I worry about; it's the gradual decay of mental power. At least you're aware of arthritis when you have it. When your mind begins to decay, you can only tell that you're going mentally downhill by the use of your judgment, which is itself a function of your decaying mind. How many people must be senile and be too senile to tell that they're senile."

Inevitably, our eyes shifted to Griswold, who occupied his usual chair, with his white hair framing his pink and relatively unlined face and his thick white mustache just faintly moist with the last visit of the scotch and soda he had in his hand.

Griswold's eyes remained closed, but he said, "From the talk about senility and the sudden silence, I gather you are all concentrating your feeble minds on me. It won't help you. You may all be admiring my powerful mind, but none of you will ever have one like it for yourself. Of course, we may have immortality someday, or at least potential immortality. In fact, we might already have had it in our own time except that—except that—"

He seemed to be drifting off, but I nudged him gently awake. Actually, what I really did was stamp on his shoe. He said, "Ouch!" and his eyes opened.

"What's this about immortality?" I said.

I cannot vouch [said Griswold] for the story I am about to tell you. If it were something I had personally witnessed and experienced, you could, of course, be sure of its absolute veracity and thorough reliability. The essential parts of this story, however, were told me by a stranger a couple of years ago and I can't be sure about it. He may have been attempting to practice on my credulity, which people often do because they judge from my frank and open countenance that I can be imposed upon. Of course, they learn better quickly.

I met the gentleman I speak of in a bar. I was passing the time in Chicago waiting for a plane that would be taking me to Atlanta on business that has nothing whatever to do with the matter at hand, and sitting on the stool next to me was a fellow who had the subtle appearance of being about to go to seed. His jacket had the beginnings of wrinkles, his jowls the beginnings of stubble, his shoes the beginnings of scuff marks. And he looked sad.

He caught my eye and raised his drink to me. He had the beginnings of intoxication. Just the beginnings. He was just sufficiently far gone to talk to strangers. He said, "To you, sir. You have a kind face." He sipped a bit, and so did I, and then he said, "I am sorry you will have to grow old and die, and that I will, and that everyone will. I drink to the needlessly aging people the whole world over."

He had the sound of an educated man and the non-sense he was saying made just enough sense to make me curious to hear more. I said, "Will you join me at a table, sir, so that we can discuss the matter privately? And will you permit the next round to be on me?"

"Certainly, sir," he said with alacrity, descending briskly from the stool. "You are a noble fellow."

Well, I am, of course, so I could see that drink had not yet incapacitated his judgment. We sat together at a corner table in a largely empty bar and he began talking at once. He heaved an enormous sigh and said, "I am a chemist. My name is Brooke. Simon Brooke. I received my doctorate from Wisconsin."

"Good afternoon, Dr. Brooke," I said gravely. "I am Griswold."

He said, "I worked with Lucas J. Atterbury. I assume you never heard of him."

"I never did."

"My own feeling is that he was probably the greatest biochemist in the world. He had no formal training in the field and I suspect he never even finished college, but he had a natural flair. Things turned to gold in his fingers as soon as he touched them. Do you know what I mean?"

I knew what he meant.

"You could go to college," said Brooke thoughtfully, "as I did and you would then know all the ways in which a problem could be studied and all the reasons why it couldn't be solved—and Lucas (he wouldn't let anyone call him by anything but his first name) who didn't know all those things would just sit in his chair and think and come up with something that would be just right.

I said, "He must have been worth millions to anyone with problems."

"You'd think so, wouldn't you? Well, that wasn't Lucas's way. He didn't want to solve just any problems that were handed to him, except once in a while just to earn some handsome fees that would keep him in funds and allow him to work on the one problem that interested him."

"Which was?"

"Immortality. He was seventy-seven when I met him and he had been working on that for seventeen years; ever since he was sixty and had decided that he had to do something to keep his life in existence past his normal life expectancy. By the time he was seventy-seven he was in the last stages of annoyance with himself. If he had started when he was fifty, you see, he could have solved the problem in time, but he hadn't felt the approach of old age till it was perhaps too late.

"So, when he was seventy-seven, he was sufficiently desperate to hire an assistant. I was the assistant. It wasn't the sort of job I wanted, but he offered me a decent salary and I thought I could use it as a stepping-stone to something else. I sneered at him as an uneducated tinkerer at first—but he caught me. When he talked to me about his theories, he used all the wrong terminology, but eventually it seemed to make sense.

"He thought that with me doing much of the experimentation, he might still make it before he died, so he kept me working hard. And the whole project became important to me.

"You see—old age is programmed into our genes. There are inevitable changes that go on in the cells, changes that put an end to them finally. The changes clog them, stiffen them, disorder them. If you can find out exactly what the changes are and how to reverse them or, better yet, prevent them, we'd live for as long as we want to and stay young forever."

I said, "If it's built into our cells, then old age and death must have a reason for existence and perhaps shouldn't be tampered with."

"Of course there's a reason for it," said Brooke. "You can't have evolution without the periodic replacement of the old generation by the new. It's just that we don't need that anymore. Science is at the brink of being able to direct evolution.

"In any case, Lucas had discovered what the crucial change was. He had found the chemical basis for old age and he was seeking for a way to reverse it, some chemical or physical treatment that would reverse that change.

The treatment, properly administered, would be the fountain of youth.''

"How did you know he had discovered it?"

"I have more than a statement. I was with him four years and in that time I had mice that showed the effects. I could inject an old mouse at his instructions, one that was clearly on the point of death from old age, and that mouse would take on the attributes of youth before my eyes.''

"Then it was all done.''

"Not quite. The mouse would grow young, frolic about in the joy of youth and then, after a day or two, it would die. There were clearly undesirable side effects to the treatment and Lucas had not, at first, managed to do away with them. That was his final task.—But he never gave me any details. I worked under instructions without ever knowing *exactly* what was happening. It was his mania for secrecy. He wanted everything under his control. So when the time came that he had solved the problem, it was too late.''

"In what way?''

"On the day he had solved the problem, he was in his eighty-second year and he had a stroke. It was on that very day—the excitement I'm sure. He could barely talk and was clearly dying. When the doctors gave him a moment to himself, he motioned to me feebly. 'I have it,' he whispered with an articulation I could barely make out. 'Carry on. Preparations D-27, D-28. To be mixed but only after held overnight at—at—' His voice grew feebler. 'At forty degrees—'

"I couldn't make out the final mumble, but I knew the only things that could come after 'forty degrees.' I said, 'Fahrenheit or Celsius.' He mumbled again and said, 'Do it today or it won't, won't—' I said again urgently, 'Fahrenheit or Celsius.' He mumbled again and said, 'Do it today or it won't, won't—' I said again urgently, and lapsed into a coma. He never came out of it and died the next day.

"And there I was. I had two unstable solutions that would not last through the day. If I could mix them properly and inject myself—I was ready for the risk if it meant the chance of immortality—I could then live long enough to rediscover the secret for general use. Or at least *I* could stay young forever. But I didn't know the key point about the preparation—the temperature.''

''Is there much difference there?'' I asked.

''Certainly. A temperature of forty degrees Celsius is forty degrees above the Celsius freezing point at zero degrees. Every ten Celsius degrees is equal to eighteen Fahrenheit degrees so forty Celsius degrees above freezing is four times eighteen, or seventy-two Fahrenheit degrees above freezing. But the Fahrenheit freezing point is at thirty-two degrees Fahrenheit, and thirty-two plus seventy-two is one hundred and four. Therefore, forty degrees Celsius is equal to one hundred and four degrees Fahrenheit.

''Now, then, did I use forty degrees Fahrenheit, which is quite cool or forty degrees Celsius, which is quite warm. Hot or cold? I didn't know. I couldn't make up my mind, so the two solutions lost their potency and I lost my chance forever.''

I said, ''Didn't you know which scale Lucas customarily used?''

''Scientists use Celsius exclusively,'' said Brooke, ''but Lucas wasn't really a trained scientist. He used whichever one appealed to him at the time. One could never be sure.''

''What did he mean, 'doesn't matter'?''

''I don't know. He was dying. I assume he felt life slipping away and nothing mattered anymore. Damn it, why couldn't he have spoken a little more clearly. Imagine! The secret of immortality, and all of it lost in a mumble that didn't clearly distinguish between Fahrenheit and Celsius.''

Brooke, who was quite drunk now, didn't realize how bad it was, for of course the dying man's instructions were perfectly clear, as you have probably seen for yourselves.

Griswold adjusted his position in his chair as though to drop off again, but Baranov seized his wrist and said,

"Are you trying to tell me you know which temperature scale this Lucas was referring to?"

"Of course," said Griswold, indignantly. "It's obvious. If you say 'forty degrees mumble, mumble' those mumbles don't have to be either 'Fahrenheit' or 'Celsius.' There's a third alternative."

"Which?" I asked.

"He could be saying 'forty degrees below zero.' "

"Even if he did," said Jennings, "we still wouldn't know if it were Fahrenheit or Celsius."

"Yes we would," said Griswold. "You've heard that forty Celsius degrees is equal to seventy-two Fahrenheit degrees. That means that forty Celsius degrees below zero degrees Celsius, which is the Celsius freezing point, is seventy-two degrees below thirty-two degrees Fahrenheit, which is the Fahrenheit freezing point. But seventy-two degrees below the thirty-two-mark is forty degrees below zero degrees Fahrenheit.

"Therefore, forty degrees below zero Celsius is forty degrees below zero Fahrenheit. If you say 'forty degrees below zero,' it doesn't matter whether it's Celsius or Fahrenheit and that's the *only* temperature where it doesn't matter. That's why Lucas said, 'doesn't matter.'

"Well, Brooke never saw that little point and I don't think that he has the brains to rediscover the treatment, or that anyone will in our lifetimes. So we'll just continue to grow old."

The Thirteenth Page

There was a rather despairing air about this particular evening at the Union Club. I had been glancing over the front page of the paper and tossed it to one side in disgust.

Baranov said, reading my mind without difficulty, "There just isn't anything new to say or do about the hostage situation in Iran." He faded out, after having delivered himself of that useless comment.

"I wish," said Jennings wistfully, "that we had withdrawn everyone at our embassy the week before the takeover. We should have. I imagine it was a failure of Intelligence that we didn't."

"Fooey," I said. "Who needs spies and secret messages for an open-and-shut case like that. We knew the Iranian mood; we knew we were treating the Shah in New York. We should have—"

Now at last Griswold opened one eye and glared at me. "Damn fool," he muttered. "If you don't know anything, why talk? There was no reason to expect a flagrant breach of international law like that when even the Nazis always behaved correctly in that respect. Then, too, you can't carry an evacuation through at a moment's notice. It would take time and careful preparation and if we went about it and the Iranian mob, very well orchestrated by the way, then took over, everyone would have said that the hostages were taken only because we had tried to evacuate the embassy. Of course, as Jennings said, our Intelligence capacity was not exactly utilized to capacity."

Jennings smiled. "Then you admit that Intelligence can fail."

"Certainly," said Griswold, lifting his scotch and soda to his lips and then wiping his white mustache delicately, "now that I've retired. There were failures even when I was active, under unusual circumstances, as when I wasn't called in soon enough. For instance—"

I have always maintained [said Griswold] that it was the English language that allowed the Tet offensive to be such a surprise. Militarily, it was the turning point of the Vietnam war. It destroyed President Johnson politically; it broke the faith of the American people in victory; it made an eventual evacuation inevitable. And all because one person was proud of his knowledge of English and others wouldn't listen.

You have to understand the difficulties that lie in the way of working with secret messages. Even if a message represents a true estimate of the situation and has safely been sent off, will it be intercepted? If it is not intercepted, will it be correctly interpreted? If it is correctly interpreted, will it be believed? Stalin's spies in Germany in early 1941 kept him perfectly up to date on Hitler's plans for an attack on the Soviet Union, for instance. Stalin simply refused to believe the reports.

Then, too, the art of decoding messages has enforced such complexity upon the mechanics of cryptography that the weight of precaution can break down the process.

For instance, there are some systems of cryptography that follow the solution to the puzzle of the perfect solvent, the material that is supposed to dissolve all substances. The problem in the case of such a solvent is: what do you use for a container?

Actually there are two solutions. One is to saturate the perfect solvent with glass and when it can dissolve no more, you can safely use a glass container. What if you need pure solvent, however, without glass or anything else dissolved in it?

In that case, you reason that the solvent must be formed in the first place, for no naturally occurring material is a perfect solvent. Therefore, you carry the formation through to the point where you have two substances which are each themselves unremarkable but which, on mixing, will give you the perfect solvent. You keep each in a separate container and when you are ready to use the perfect solvent, you add some of each component to the material you want dissolved. The perfect solvent forms at the site of use and dissolves the material.

You see the analogy. In cryptography, you can send two messages, each of which is meaningless without the other. In that case, interception of one will be of no help to the enemy and of no harm to us. Interception even of both may not serve the enemy, if he doesn't appreciate the connection of the two. It also means that at least one of the messages does not have to be very obscure.

Suppose a particular message cannot be decoded without a keyword, arbitrarily selected for the occasion, and that the keyword is sent separately by another route.

If you want a keyword that is as little as ten letters long, then the number of possibilities of ten-letter combinations based on the twenty-six letters of the alphabet is almost exactly a million billion. Nobody's going to guess that combination by luck, and no one can possibly think of using force and of trying every possible combination one at a time.

How do you decide on the keyword? One way—not the only way—is to have an agreed-on book (one that is changed periodically) and choose a ten-letter combination at random out of it. You then use a small coding machine to code the message around the keyword and send the keyword itself separately. The keyword can be and sometimes is just a scrawled notation such as 73/12 indicating page 73, line 12. Look up the page and line of the book of the week and the first ten letters, or the last ten letters, or whatever you've agreed on is the key.

Either message might, for some reason, not arrive, but it is in the highest degree frustrating if both messages arrive and yet, even taken together, make no sense.

Something of that sort happened in January 1968, and it was fatal.

Here are the essential details. A message came through to Saigon headquarters from an operative in Hue. The agent who sent it was the best we had. He was a Vietnamese, heart and soul on our side, and with an excellent command of English that he ordinarily took care to hide. He actually operated with the Vietcong, so you can imagine the risks he ran.

He kept his coding machine well hidden, of course, and the books he used for determining the keyword. They were British paperback thrillers in rotation, and it was his choice. He liked them. They were literate and he ceaselessly polished his English on them. He was proud of his facility with the language—all this turned up afterward, too late—and on those occasions when he met with our men, he would trot out his full vocabulary, and go out of his way to demonstrate his knowledgeability on the matter of synonyms, idioms, ambiguities and so on. Our men, being native to the language, didn't know it nearly as well and, I imagine, listened with impatience or, I strongly suspect, didn't listen at all—a terrible mistake.

The key arrived and seemed perfectly clear. Stripped of the red herrings with which it was routinely surrounded, it read "13 THP/2NDL" which was interpreted, quite reasonably, as the thirteenth page and second line. That was turned to in the book, the first ten letters taken, and fed into the computer. The message was then inserted and what came out was garblement, absolute chaos and meaninglessness.

They were astonished, and I imagine they tried it several times before being satisfied that something was wrong. They decided that, through some error, the agent had used the wrong book. They sent a message back to Hue in order to get a confirmation. That meant the loss of time. When they got back nothing, they sent an army officer and I suppose you can imagine what he found.

The agent had disappeared the morning after the message had been sent out. He has never been heard of again as far as I know, so that we can assume the

Vietcong finally discovered the game he had been playing. As I said, it was January 1968, and considering what was about to happen, the enemy must have been highly sensitive to all sorts of things.

Well, then, what to do with the message? It didn't work and it wasn't ever going to work. The people at Saigon were quite convinced on that point.

They were therefore faced with two alternatives. The first was simply to ignore it. If a message were intercepted and you never received it, there was nothing to be done, and operationally this fell into the same category. It might just as well never have been received.

However, it *was* received. The receipt was on record. And if it carried an important communication—as, in point of fact, it did, though no one knew it at the time—someone would have to be blamed, and whoever made the decision to ignore the matter would be the candidate. The people at Saigon had a healthy resistance to the notion of being scapegoated, and looked for a second alternative.

They found one. One of the operatives had a month's leave coming and had in any case intended to whoop it up in the United States for a while. He went, took the message with him, and brought it to Washington. Carefully, he placed it in the lap of the Department and it was their baby now.

The Department was as helpless as the Saigon people were. They brooded over it, discussed it, dared not throw it away lest it be *their* butt in a sling—and they, unlike the Saigon people, had no one to whom to pass the buck.

Two entire weeks passed before someone finally took the chance of saying, "Let's ask Griswold!"

I can understand the hesitation. They knew my opinion of the Vietnam war and they had the definite feeling I wasn't to be trusted in matters relating to it. But now they had nowhere else to turn. If they had only understood that as little as three days before.

They found me, brought me in, and put the entire case before me. What they wanted me to say was that in my expert opinion they might as well consider it a garbled message; that you can't get something out of nothing; and to forget it. Then, if the worst came to the worst, it would be *my* skin that would be separated from *my* body.

Before I got into that position, however, I demanded to see the man from Vietnam, who was still in the country.

I said, "Tell me about the Hue agent, the one who disappeared. Are you sure he was captured and to be presumed dead? Are you sure he wasn't Vietcong all the time; that he finally didn't decide he had had enough, sent off nonsense and joined his friends?"

"No, no," said the other, "I don't think that's possible at all. His wife and children had been killed in North Vietnam rather atrociously and he wanted his revenge. Besides—" he grinned, "he had a thing about his command of the English language. Sometimes I think that held him to us more than anything else. He might desert us, he might forget his passion for revenge, but he would never give up the chance of lecturing Americans and Englishmen on their own language. Not that we listened, of course. On the few occasions I met with him clandestinely, he was unbearably tedious on the subject."

"For instance?"

"I scarcely remember. He always said that all languages were ambiguous, but that native speakers were so used to the ambiguities they never paid attention. Like that."

"Did he give examples?"

"I don't remember."

"Well now, we have here '13 THP/2NDL' for thirteenth page, second line. Why the extra letters? Wouldn't '13/2' have been enough?"

"Hey," said the man from Vietnam, "he always did use that combination, but your questions have reminded me. He claimed *that* was ambiguous."

"The 13/2?"

"Yes."

"Why?"

"He didn't say—I don't think he said."

"So he sent it off in this version to prove it was ambiguous?"

"I don't see that. It's the same thing, with or without the letters. Thirteenth page, second line."

"Not at all," I said, and explained. He stared at me as though I were crazy.

I was right, of course. With the new key, the message decoded beautifully, and the full details of the forthcoming Tet offensive lay before us.

Except it wasn't forthcoming; it took place on that very day and we were caught flat-footed.

"But what are you talking about?" I demanded in astonishment as Griswold returned to his drink and seemed to lapse into deep thought. "What did the phrase mean if not '13th page, 2nd line'?"

Griswold said, "No problem. That's what it meant. And they were using the right book. It was just that the agent realized the phrase was ambiguous and lent itself to misinterpretation. And with a little thought I could see what he meant, as I think anyone should."

"But *I* don't," I said.

"So think a little. The lines on a page aren't numbered so '2nd line' means 'line 2' counting from the top in the conventional way. No problem. However, pages *are* numbered and *that* produces the confusion since '13th page' is not necessarily 'page 13.' "

Baranov said quite loudly, "Griswold, you've finally come apart. What else can '13th page' be but 'page 13'?"

Griswold said, "I notice you have a paperback in your jacket pocket, so we don't have to send for one. Would you take it out and turn to the first page of the novel? Got it? That's the first page? Very good. Is it page 1?"

Baranov said in a very small voice, "Well, no, it's page 9."

"Exactly," said Griswold. "In paperbacks they start counting the pages at the very beginning and work their way through title page, acknowledgment, chapter headings, dedications and so on. They don't actually number the pages till the novel actually begins. The first page of the novel itself can therefore be numbered 5, 7, 9, 11—depending on how many preliminary pages were used up.

"In that case, you see, page 13 is the 13th page of the book, but not at all the 13th page of the novel it contains. This was what the Hue agent had eating at him and that he tried to explain and that no one would listen to. So he stubbornly used '13th page' to indicate he did not mean 'page 13,' but the thirteenth page of that particular novel, which happened to fall on page 21. When they used the keyword from the first letters of the 2nd line on that page, they got the message—but too late."

1 to 999

One can't help getting tired of Griswold at times. At least I can't.

I like him well enough. I can't help liking the old fraud, with his infinite capacity to hear in his sleep and his everlasting sipping at his scotch and soda, and his lies, and his scowls at us from under his enormous white eyebrows. But if I could catch him at his lies only once I think I would like him a lot better.

Of course, he might be telling the truth, but surely there can't be any one person in the world to whom so many impossible problems are posed. I don't believe it! I *don't* believe it.

I sat there that night in the Union Club with windy gusts of rain battering the windows now and then, and the traffic on Park Avenue rather muted and I suppose my thoughts must have been spoken aloud.

At least, Jennings said, "What don't you believe?"

I was caught a little by surprise, but I jerked my thumb in Griswold's direction. "Him!" I said. "Him!"

I half expected Griswold to growl back at me at that, but he seemed peacefully asleep between the wings of his tall armchair, his white mustache moving in and out to his regular breathing.

"Come on," said Baranov. "You enjoy listening to him."

"That's beside the point," I said. "Think of all those deathbed hints, for instance. Come on! How many times do people die and leave mysterious clues to their murderers? I don't think it has ever happened even once in real life, but it happens to Griswold all the time—according to Griswold. It's an insult to expect us to believe it."

It was at that point that Griswold opened one icy-blue eye, and said, "The most remarkable deathbed clue I ever encountered had nothing to do with murder at all. It was a natural death and a deliberate joke of a sort, but I don't want to irritate you with the story." He opened his other eye and lifted his glass to his lips.

"Go ahead," said Jennings. "We are interested. We two, at least."

I was also, to be truthful—

What I am about to relate [said Griswold] involved no crime, no police, no spies, no secret agents. There was no reason why I should have known anything about it, but one of the senior men involved knew of my reputation. I can't imagine how such a thing comes about, since I never speak of the little things I have done, for I have better things to do than advertise my prowess. It's just that others talk, things get around, and any puzzle within a thousand miles is referred to me—which is the simple reason I encounter so many. [He glared at me.]

I was not made aware of the event till it was just about over so I must tell you most of the story as it was told to me, with appropriate condensation, of course, for I am not one to linger unnecessarily over details.

I will not name the institute at which it all took place or tell you where it is or when it happened. That would give you a chance to check my veracity and I consider it damned impertinent that any of you should feel it required checking or that you should go about snuffling after evidence.

In this unnamed institute there were people who dealt with the computerization of the human personality. What they wanted to do was to construct a program that would enable a computer to carry on a conversation that would be indistinguishable from that of a human being. Something like that has been done in the case of psychoanalytic double-talk, where a computer is designed to play the role of a Freudian who repeats his patient's remarks. That is trivial. What the institute was after was creative small talk, the swapping of ideas.

I was told that no one at the institute really expected to accomplish the task, but the mere attempt to do so was sure to uncover much of interest about the human mind, about human emotions and personality.

No one made much progress in this matter except for Horatio Trombone—obviously, I have just invented that name and there is no use your trying to track it down.

Trombone had been able to make a computer do remarkable things, to respond in a fairly human fashion for a good length of time. No one would have mistaken it for a human being, of course, but Trombone did far better than anyone else had done, so there was considerable curiosity as to the nature of his program.

Trombone, however, would not divulge any information on the matter. He kept absolutely silent. He worked alone, without assistants or secretaries. He went so far as to burn all but the most essential records and keep those in a private safe. His intention, he said, was to keep matters strictly to himself until he himself was satisfied with what he had accomplished. He would then reveal all and accumulate the full credit and adulation that he was sure he deserved. One gathered he expected the Nobel Prize to begin with and to go straight uphill from there.

This struck others at the institute, you can well imagine, as eccentricity carried to the point of insanity, which may have been what it was. If he were mad, however, he was a mad genius and his superiors were reluctant to interfere with him. Not only did they feel that, left to himself, he might produce shattering scientific breakthroughs, but none of them had any hankering to go down in the science-history books as a villain.

Trombone's immediate superior, whom I will call Herbert Bassoon, argued with his difficult underling now and then. "Trombone," he would say, "if we could have a number of people combining mind and thought on this, progress would go faster."

"Nonsense," Trombone would say irascibly. "One

intelligent person doesn't go faster just because twenty fools are nipping at his heels. You only have one decently intelligent person here, other than myself, and if I die before I'm done, he can carry on. I will leave him my records, but they will go only to him, and not until I die.''

Trombone usually chuckled at such times, I was told, for he had a sense of humor as eccentric as his sense of privacy, and Bassoon told me that he had a premonition of just such trouble as eventually took place—though that may very well have been only hindsight.

The chance of Trombone's dying was, unfortunately, all too good, for his heart was pumping on hope alone. There had been three heart attacks and there was a general opinion that the fourth would kill him. Nevertheless, though he was aware of the precarious thread by which his life hung, he would never name the one person he thought a worthy successor. Nor, by his actions, was it possible to judge who it might be. Trombone seemed to be amused at keeping the world in ignorance.

The fourth heart attack came while he was at work and it did kill him. He was alone at the time so there was no one to help him. It didn't kill him at once and he had time to feed instructions to his computer. At least, the computer produced a printout, which was found at the time his body was.

Trombone also left a will in the possession of his lawyer who made its terms perfectly clear. The lawyer had the combination to the safe that held Trombone's records and that combination was to be released to no one but Trombone's chosen successor. The lawyer did not have the name of the successor, but the will stated that there would be an indication left behind. If people were too stupid to understand it—those were the words in the will—then, after the space of one week, all his records were to be destroyed.

Bassoon argued strenuously that the public good counted for more than Trombone's irrational orders; that his dead hand must not interfere with the advance of science. The lawyer, however, was adamant; long before the law could move, the records would be destroyed, since any legal action was to be at once met with destruction according to the terms of the will.

There was nothing to do but turn to the printout, and what it contained was a series of numerals: 1, 2, 3, 4 and so on, all the numerals up to 999. The series was carefully scanned. There was not one numeral missing, not one out of place; the full list, 1 to 999.

Bassoon pointed out that the instructions for such a printout were very simple, something Trombone might have done even at the point of death. Trombone might have intended something more complicated than a mere unbroken list of numerals, but had not had a chance to complete the instruction. Therefore, Bassoon said, the printout was not a true indication of what was in Trombone's mind and the will was invalid.

The lawyer shrugged that off. It was mere speculation, he said. In the absence of evidence to the contrary, the printout had to be taken as it appeared, as saying exactly what Trombone wanted it to say.

Bassoon gathered his staff together for a meeting of minds. There were twenty men and women, any one of whom could, conceivably, have carried on Trombone's work. Every one of them would have longed for the chance, but no one of them could advance any logical bit of evidence that he or she was the one Trombone thought to be the "one decently intelligent person" among them. At least, not one could convince any of the others that he or she was the person.

Nor could a single one see any connection between that dull list of numerals and any person in the institute. I imagine some invented theories, but none were convincing to them all generally, and certainly none were convincing to the lawyer or moved him in any way.

Bassoon was slowly going mad. On the last day of the grace period, when he was no nearer a solution than at the start, he turned to me. I received his call at a time when I was very busy, but I knew Bassoon slightly, and I have always found it difficult to refuse help—especially to someone who sounded as desperate as he did.

We met in his office and he looked wretched. He told

me the whole story and said when he had finished, "It is maddening to have what may be an enormous advance in that most difficult of subjects—the working of the human mind—come to nothing because of a half-mad eccentric, a stubborn robot of a lawyer and a silly piece of paper. Yet I can make nothing of it."

I said, "Can it be a mistake to concentrate on the numerals? Is there anything unusual about the paper itself?"

"I swear to you, no," he said energetically. "It was ordinary paper without a mark on it except for the numerals from 1 to 999. We've done everything except subject it to neutron activation analysis, and I think I'd do that if I thought it would help. If you think I ought to, I will, but surely you can do better than that. Come on, Griswold; you have the reputation of being able to solve any puzzle."

I don't know where he got that notion. I never discuss such things myself.

I said, "There isn't much time—"

"I know," he said, "but I'll show you the paper; I'll introduce you to all the people who might be involved. I'll give you any information you need, any help you want—but we only have seven hours."

"Well," I said, "we may only need seven seconds. I don't know the names of the twenty people who might qualify as Trombone's successor, but if one of them has a rather unusual first name I have in mind—though it might conceivably be a surname—then I should say that is the person you are looking for."

I told him the name I had in mind and he jumped. It was unusual and one of the people at the institute did bear it. Even the lawyer admitted that person must be the intended successor, when I explained my reasoning, so the records were passed over.

However, I don't believe anything much has come of the research after all, unfortunately. In any case, that's the story.

"No, it isn't," I exploded. "What was the name you suggested and how did you get it out of a list of numerals from 1 to 999."

Griswold, who had returned placidly to his drink, looked up sharply. "I can't believe you don't see it," he said. "The numerals went from 1 to 999 without missing a numeral and then stopped. I asked myself what the numerals from 1 to 999 inclusive had in common that numerals higher still, say 1000, do not have, and how that can have anything to do with some one particular person.

"As written, I saw nothing, but suppose all those numerals were written out as English words: one, two, three, four and so on, all the way up to nine hundred ninety-nine. That list of numbers is constructed of letters, but not of all twenty-six letters. Some letters are not to be found in the words for the first 999 numbers; letters, such as 'a,' 'b,' 'c,' 'j,' 'k,' 'm,' 'p.'

"The most remarkable of these is 'a.' It is the third most commonly used letter in the English language with only 'e' and 't' ahead of it, yet you may go through all the numbers—one, fifty-three, seven hundred eighty-one, and you will not find a single 'a.' Once you pass 999, however, it breaks down. The number 1000, 'one thousand,' has an 'a' but not any of the other missing letters. It seems quite clear, then, that the message hidden behind the list is simply the absence of 'a.' What's so difficult about that?"

I said, angrily, "That's just nonsense. Even if we were to admit that the message was the absence of 'a,' what would that mean as far as the successor was concerned? A name that lacked any 'a'?"

Griswold gave me a withering look. "I thought there would be several names like that and there were. But I also thought that some one person might have the name 'Noah,' which is pretty close to 'no a' and one of them did. How much simpler can it be?"

Twelve Years Old

Jennings was a little testy as he walked into the Union Club that evening. He was the last to join us.

"Right now," he said, as he lowered himself into his chair and raised his hand to signify his inevitable dry martini, "what I would most like to do is hand my kid nephew a juicy one, or maybe six, in the seat of his pants."

"He's annoying, is he?" said Baranov.

"Is Mount St. Helens annoying? That little penny dreadful has the damndest habit of being right in little ways and sneering at you. I don't mind a kid being bright, but he doesn't have to make a career out of humiliating everyone in sight."

"Twelve years old, I take it," I said.

"Yes. How did you know?" said Jennings.

I sighed. "Look, I'm a professional lecturer and in the question-and-answer session I watch out for possible troublemakers and don't call on them. Any time I miscalculate and some undersized runt with sharp features and a boy-soprano voice asks a particularly embarrassing question, I say, 'You're twelve years old, I take it' and they always answer 'Yes, how did you know?'"

"What is this?" said Jennings grumpily. "A cosmic rule?"

"Apparently," I said. "Before they're twelve, they haven't accumulated enough irritating knowledge. After they're twelve, they've had some sense and judgment knocked into them. *At* twelve, they're unbearable. Listen, I was once a twelve-year-old unbearable myself."

"You still are," said Baranov gently.

I ignored that with the contempt it deserved and said, "Ask Griswold. I'll bet he agrees with me."

Griswold seemed, to all appearances, restfully asleep in his armchair, but we knew better.

He stirred, brought his scotch and soda to his lips, brushed his white mustache and said, "Bright twelve-year-olds are cooperative enough if you can convince them you are their intellectual equal. Naturally, this puts the three of you behind the eight ball. In my own case, however—"

Jennings said feelingly, "If you met my nephew—"

In my own case [said Griswold, raising his voice somewhat, and opening his ice-blue eyes] I manage well.

It was a matter that took place a couple of years ago. A Middle-Eastern diplomat was shot down in the streets of suburban Washington and it might have been an ordinary mugging, but the Department didn't think so.

It's become commonplace to have the internal warfare of any nation in turmoil fought out on the streets of nations that have little or nothing to do with the matter directly. It's extremely difficult to do anything about it, too. Even when there's evidence that can be used—which isn't often—there are almost always diplomatic considerations involved.

On the one hand, we can't condone terrorist activity or political assassinations within our borders. On the other hand, we don't want to introduce unnecessary complexities in sensitive relationships with other powers.

Just the same, you at least want to know what really happened so that you can make whatever move you decide is most judicious under the circumstances out of a correct knowledge, and not out of guesses. There have been cases when we acted out of insufficient knowledge and landed neatly in the diplomatic soup—or in an embarrassing position vis-à-vis American public opinion.

The assassination I speak of (and I can't go into detail because, for various important security reasons, the thing was pretty much hushed up) was a particularly sensitive one and, fortunately, there was a witness. In a way, it was the best kind of witness. One pair of eyes had been at a window and they belonged to a bright twelve-year-old.

There was no question but that he had seen exactly what had happened and that he would be able to describe it in full and accurate detail.

The assassins could not have known the formidable character of the witness, but they were desperate enough to take no chances. They sent a bullet through the window when they saw him there, and missed. Over the next couple of days, two other attempts were made on his life and failed, and then the youngster—I'll call him Eli—was taken into custody. Guards were placed on his home.

There was a catch. Eli wouldn't talk.

I was already in retirement, so I wasn't directly involved, but Jerry Bastwell came to see me, muttering under his breath and mopping at his bald head.

"That little bastard," he said. "He just sits there and laughs at us. He says, 'You don't want to know. You'll just mess it up, anyhow.' "

I said, "Did you talk to his parents? Let them ask the questions."

"His parents!" said Jerry with disgust. "They say they can't handle him. They say he's very bright and reads at a high school level and is getting private tutoring for college entrance, and they can't handle him. I think they're afraid of him.—Sounds like a wise-guy dumb kid to me. Less tutoring and special treatment, and a little more slamming around would do him a lot of good and knock some of the crap out of him."

"So, slam him around," I said. "Give him the third degree and knock the crap out of him."

Jerry was not one to understand heavy irony when he heard it. "We can't," he said. "The kid's got a psychiatrist who says if we put pressure on him, he'll retreat into silence. He says the kid has autistic tendencies, whatever that means. We have to treat him carefully."

"Why are you telling me all this?" I asked.

"Some of the people at the Department think *you* ought to talk to him. You've got a way with you, some kind of a—a—"

"Peculiar mind? Set a nut to catch a nut?"

Jerry sighed with relief. "I wasn't sure how to put it, but that's it."

It was exactly the kind of compliment designed to set me going. I was curious about the youngster and I agreed to see him.

He was thin and undersized and moved with quick restlessness as is characteristic of bright twelve-year-olds. The world just doesn't get out of the way quickly enough and they're impatient. He gave me a contemptuous sneer. "You coming to ask questions, too?"

"Maybe," I said, sitting down. "Mostly I'm interested in you."

"Why?"

"Because I think you're interesting. You know a lot, they tell me. Perhaps you can teach me something I don't know."

"You know anything about cosmogony?"

"Well," I said cautiously, "it's one of the few words with 'o' as the only vowel. 'Cosmology' and 'lobotomy' are two others." That was merely intended as a light-hearted way of indicating ignorance, but he caught me up at once.

"There are 'y's' in those words and that counts as a vowel. 'Colophon' is a better example of an 'o'-only word. 'Syzygy' has three 'y's' as the only vowels. You interested in words?"

I said, "Very much so."

"We're lucky to have the English language," said Eli very seriously. "That's got the most words of any language and the spelling is crazy so you can have fun with it. Hardly anyone knows anything about spelling these days, but I won an all-school spelling bee when I was seven."

"I'm pretty good at spelling," I said.

He said, "Spell 'sizum.' "

I said, "s-c-h-i-s-m. The 'ch' is silent, although some dictionaries say it doesn't have to be and you can say 'skizm.' "

Eli nodded vigorously. "In English," he said, "s-c-h at the start is almost always pronounced 's-k' like, for instance, schedule, scheme, schizophrenia, school, scholar, schooner, Schenectady and Schuyler.''

I said, ''How about schlemiel, schlock and wiener schnitzel?''

He let out a squawk of laughter. ''Those aren't English words. They're loan words from Yiddish or German.''

I said, ''The British pronounce schedule as 'shedule.' ''

''They're crazy,'' said Eli flatly. ''I heard an Englishman on a television program once who said 'school schedule' and pronounced it just the way you said, 'skool shedule.' Both words start with 'sch' so why didn't he pronounce it 'school schedule.' ''

''Well, that's the English language, Eli. As you said, the spelling is crazy, but the pronunciation is crazy, too. Did you ever throw a dollar bill from one room into another.''

For a moment, he stared at me suspiciously. ''Why do you ask?''

''Because if you did, I could say that you tossed dough through a door. That's 'doh throo,' right, even though the words each end in 'ough'. Why don't I say 'tossed doh throh' or 'tossed doo throo'?''

He laughed and looked friendly for the first time. ''That's nice. Do you mind if I use that?''

''Of course not.''

He bounced up out of his chair, walked rapidly toward me and poked me in the chest with his finger. ''Listen, I've got a puzzle for you.''

''Good,'' I said, careful to show no irritation at the poke though his fingernail was sharp, and it hurt. ''Then it will be my turn.''

''You've got a puzzle, too?''

''Sort of. A puzzle about murder. You ask me your question about your puzzle, then I'll ask you my question about my puzzle. And if I give you the correct answer, you'll have to give *me* the correct answer. Fair enough?''

He fell silent, considered me owlishly, then said, ''That's not the same kind of puzzle.''

''You're right,'' I said, ''but we're not the same kind

of people. You're young and quick and energetic, and I'm old and slow and tired, so you've got your kind of puzzle and I've got mine, and if I can handle yours, you can surely handle mine.''

He considered a little longer, then said, ''All right. It's a deal,'' and he stuck his hand out at me. I shook it gravely and then he said, ''Besides you won't get this.''

''Try me,'' I said with a smile.

He said, ''I'll bet I can write out a word in capital letters, and you can't pronounce it.''

''Is that the one where you show me a word and I pronounce the word you show me and you say, 'No, I said you can't pronounce *it*' and the word 'it' is pronounced 'it,' of course.''

Eli made a face. ''That's a silly-kid sort of thing. I really mean there's a word you can't pronounce. It's a short, very familiar word and everyone sees it all the time. And I'm not going to show it to you, either. What I'm saying is that if I were to write this short very familiar word in capital letters, you won't be able to pronounce that word I show you.''

''How am I going to pronounce the word if you don't show it to me?

''Because you're going to have to guess what the word is. What word is unpronounceable even though it's written out clearly in capital letters and isn't very long and isn't very complicated?''

''And if I tell you, will you answer my questions?''

''Yes.''

So I told him and he crowed with laughter and bounced into my lap and hugged me out of sheer relief, I imagine, at having found an adult with a wit as quick as his own.

After that, he told us all we wanted to know and we had a particular embassy do a bit of house cleaning and had some private no-nonsense conversations with a particular power. It wasn't much, but it was all we could conveniently do. It won't keep them quiet forever, I'm sure, but it's kept them quiet so far.

I said ominously, ''You know you're not going to get away without telling us the unpronounceable word.''

Griswold looked at me with contempt. He said, "Lend me your pen." He reached for the memo pad on the table on his right and carefully wrote "polish" upon it and said, "Pronounce it."

I did and said, "What's the catch? I pronounce it every time I ask someone to polish my shoes."

"There's no problem when it's in lower case. Eli said three times I couldn't pronounce it if it were written in capitals. He emphasized the capitals."

Baranov protested, "But writing it in capitals doesn't change the pronunciation." He wrote "POLISH" under Griswold's "polish" on the memo pad.

Griswold said, "You're quite wrong. There's no way of being sure of how to pronounce 'POLISH' in capital letters because you can't tell if it's a capitalized word or not. When all the letters are capitals, you can't tell the condition of the first letter. In the English language, one word that changes pronunciation on capitalization is 'polish' for it becomes 'Polish.' Now tell me which way you pronounce 'POLISH.' "

Testing, Testing!

There is always a sense of deep quiet at the Union Club, regardless of any hubbub that may be going on outside. The traffic sounds, the sirens, even the flashes and rumbles of a thunderstorm seem to be trapped and muffled in the immemorial drapes, leaving a hush behind that it would be sacrilege to break.

Unless, of course, you want to count the soft snoring of Griswold as he slept in his stately armchair.

Jennings eyed the sleeping figure, with its air of strange alertness-in-slumber and with the scotch and soda held rocksteady in its fingers, and said, "Do you get like that easily, I wonder?"

Baranov said, "It takes a bad break in the gene pool, I suppose."

"I mean, how do you get to be someone in his 'Department,' whatever that might be."

"He never names it," I said huffily, "and I, for one, wonder if it exists."

"Well, suppose it exists," said Jennings. "How did he get to work with it? How did he qualify? Did he just send in a letter saying 'I want to be a puzzler-out of queer riddles'?"

"Don't you remember," I said, "that he once claimed that during World War II he had this knack of being able to detect spies—or something like that?"

"That's what he says," said Jennings, "but if you were to ask him, he'd be sure to tell you a different story. I'll bet if you ask him—"

Griswold stirred and one ice-blue eye opened. As

usual, and by some process unknown to us, he had managed to begin hearing us as soon as our conversation had veered into something that involved him. He said, "If you asked me, my answer would be a simple one. They came looking for me. *They* came looking for *me*. They had sampled my brilliance in World-War-II days, and they wanted more of it, but they were hesitant just the same. They distrusted the very brilliance they wanted."

"Why should that be?" I asked hostilely.

"Because a brilliant agent has little to do. Most of the work requires the long, patient playing of a part, and for that you need a kind of dull capacity to submerge yourself. In fact, the most successful agent I ever knew was a jackass, and it was he who tested me at the crucial point."

Griswold's voice faded off and I said, "And you passed with flying colors, I presume."

"Of course," said Griswold, starting a little and emerging again from enveloping slumber, "but since that comes as no surprise to you, there's no point in telling you about it, is there?"

"Come on," said Jennings. "Wild horses couldn't keep you from telling us about it." He looked at his wristwatch. "I'll give you fifteen seconds to start."

Griswold took only five seconds, actually.

As I told you once before [said Griswold]—and I always adhere rigidly to the truth—I had made my mark as a very young man during World War II. There were people in Washington who wanted to follow me up on this in the days immediately after the war and who wished to place me in a position where my talents could be of use to them.

I was not at all keen on this, for the life of a government-employed agent is a difficult and stultifying one. I had met a number of them and I knew. Nevertheless, I was moved somewhat by feelings of patriotism and I had no objection to serving the government in a consulting capacity, so I allowed myself to be talked into coming to Washington in order that I might be studied at closer range.

I didn't think it would be pleasant and it wasn't. The Cold War was beginning and there was considerable disarray in the internal caverns of the various departments as people were beginning to sniff out undependables. Naturally, the possession of brains stamped you at once as suspicious. An agent had to have an IQ of 120 at the very least—and at the very most, too.

Naturally, I did not get along with the older officials who tended to take a dislike to me at sight. It may surprise you who now see me as a man of great dignity and maturity—and likeability withal—but in my younger days I was rather a rebel, and the merely conventional tended to bristle at once when they saw me.

I remember being met in the halls of the Department building by a man of average height with a pink, smooth face, who was dressed as meticulously and unimaginatively as your average department-store dummy. He took one look at me, pointed his finger at me and said, "You!"

I guess I was slouching a little, but I didn't bother taking my hands out of my pockets or straightening up. I wasn't in the army. I said, as pleasantly as I could, "That's what they call me. What do they call you?"

He ignored my question and said, "Why aren't you wearing a tie and jacket?"

I said, "Because when I woke up this morning, I noticed that—son of a gun—it was summer."

"It's air-conditioned in here."

"Interesting but irrelevant, since I'm only here temporarily."

"Indeed? Give me your name and let's make sure about the 'temporarily.' "

" 'You' is good enough. I answer to that." And I walked away, whistling.

I didn't know who he was but, of course, I found out. He was the Department favorite, the most successful agent of the 1940's. And he was the jackass I mentioned earlier. He had been working in and out of Germany throughout the war, facing death daily with the courage of a lion—I'll give him that—and about the brains of a lion, too.

When he walked into a room, Senators got to their feet in respect—or they would have, if they had known who he was, but of course they didn't, for an agent's stock in trade is his anonymity.

I had heard of him, of course; we all had; but I had never met him or seen his photograph. It probably wouldn't have changed anything when I met him in the corridor, if I had known who he was, to be sure.

But then, I had other things to think of. I, and five others like me, were enduring a long crash course. We had lectures on various aspects of espionage and counterespionage—on codes and cryptograms from the Morse code to those which required computers, since the first primitive electronic computers were already in operation, and on so many other things it would weary me to remember or you to hear.

Lectures were broken into by little skits of one kind or another, and we were asked questions afterward to test our ability to observe under stress. A lecturer would talk to us for half an hour then suddenly demand how many times he had rubbed his forehead and whether he had done it with his right hand or his left.

Of course, they never caught me out on any of those things. I might have deliberately failed in order to get myself booted out of the course, but I couldn't bring myself to let them think I was a fool.

Then, one day we were told to expect a lecture by our wartime hero and in walked my friend of the corridors. He remembered me, you can be sure. He stood there in the front of the room and eyed each one of us coldly. When he came to me, he barked, "Griswold!"

"Or 'you,' " I said calmly. "Either way."

He gave me a long, hard stare and said, "You think highly of yourself, apparently."

I said, "It would be poor judgment on my part not to."

"And how are you on codes?"

"I'm not an accomplished cryptographer," I said, "but I'm as good as anyone who isn't."

He turned away from me and said to the class. "The truth is we use codes every day. We give high signs. We wink, nod, lift our eyebrows. There are gestures, expressions, vague sounds. They all mean something to someone. Some of them mean the same thing to almost everyone. A nod would mean 'yes.' A pointing finger would mean 'That!'

"Just the same, we can change meaning. We can arrange to have someone shoot a gun when we nod. Nod may mean 'yes' to almost everyone at almost every time, but it means 'shoot' to one person at a particular time.

"Of course, that means prearrangement.—But suppose no prearrangement is possible. Suppose you must send an important message without using an agreed-upon code. You must make up one that looks like gibberish so that it stumps any unauthorized person who comes upon it—or better still looks so meaningless that it is discarded. Yet the person you're sending it to must be able to interpret it.

"It's tricky. You have to be clever, but not so clever that the code you use is impenetrable, and you must have *your* man cleverer than the enemy. Back in 1943, I made use of such a device. I used it twice successfully, both times in an emergency where I had to risk everything. I overconfidently tried it a third time and the enemy penetrated it. The result was that Mussolini was snatched out of imprisonment by Skorzeny and I nearly went into imprisonment—or worse.

"I will now try that code on Griswold." He grinned at me wolfishly. "A man as brilliant as he is certain he is will have no trouble, and he will have till the end of the lecture to solve it. Naturally, he had also better pay attention to me since he will be tested on that as well. The message, Griswold, consists of seven words and I will write them out on the blackboard, one under the other."

He did so:

titter
attempt

ability
intention
capacity
invincible
invidious

"That carries a message," he said, "and the rest of you are invited to work it out. You will know beyond any doubt that you have succeeded if you find the correct answer, but I expect results only from Griswold.—You will all notice that the seven words have no obvious connected meaning in the order given or in any other. They seem to have nothing in common. There are three nouns, two adjectives, a verb and one word that can be either a verb or a noun. The initial letters spell nothing either in the order given or any other. Yet I say there's a message there."

He paused and the others in the class were furrowing their brows, looking absorbed, and in every possible way were attempting to register deep thought. I didn't bother. I just leaned back in my seat, looking bored.

He stopped in front of me and said, "I will be talking for about 45 minutes, Griswold. You have till then. Will that be enough?"

I said quite distinctly, "Titrate—is—invisible."

He said, "What?"

I said, "I've solved your little code and I'm using it to answer your question as to whether I have enough time. Titrate—is—invisible."

He turned mauve. He was pink to start with, of course. He dashed out of the room and in the hubbub that followed I explained the code to the others. I was right, but it all worked out well, for I never got the job. My friend, the hero, tabbed me as insolent, uncooperative and very likely, in his expert opinion, a Communist, so I was asked to leave the next day.

I remained a free-lancer, and did very well indeed.

Griswold grunted reminiscently and seemed to be settling himself back into sonmolence when Baranov said explosively, "But what was the message? How did the code work?"

Griswold sat up in apparent astonishment. "You don't get it? But it's obvious! You must see at a glance that the first two words on the list have three 't's' each, and the last two have three 'i's' each. Once that caught my attention, I noted that every single word had either at least one 'i' or at least one 't' or both.

"What do 'i' and 't' have in common? Well, when words are written cursively—handwriting, small letters— an 'i' or a 't' interrupts the continuing line. You must stop to dot your 'i's' and cross your 't's.' Surely you see that. (You must also dot your occasional 'j's,' but 'j' is only a modern form of 'i.') Having seen that, you must see at once that the dot of the 'i' and the crossbar of the 't' are the dots and dashes of the International Morse code.

"For each word write only the dots and dashes of the 'i's' and 't's' it contains and you have——for 'titter,' — — —for 'attempt,' • •—for 'ability,' •— —• for 'intention,' •—for 'capacity,' • • • for 'invincible' and • • • again for 'invidious.'

"In the Morse code,——• — —,— — —, • •—•, •— —•, •—, • • •, • • • spells out 'you pass,' which was at once clear proof that my analysis was correct. When our friend, the hero, asked me if I had enough time, I said 'Titrate is invisible' and if you turn that into dots and dashes you get——•— —, •, • • • or 'yes.' "

The Appleby Story

Jennings said, "Extraordinarily expensive, this white-collar crime. I don't know how many billions of dollars a year it costs us."

His words rang a little hollowly in the august confines of the Union Club library. It was a mild evening and the city was sufficiently alive so that few were so at a loss for something to do as to come to the Club—except for the four of us, of course.

Baranov said, "I don't think anyone cares much about white-collar crime. The prevailing attitude is 'as long as no one gets hurt.'"

"Yes, I know," said I indignantly, "so that some poor slob who holds up a liquor store at gunpoint and gets away with fifty dollars has the book thrown at him. And some junior-executive smoothy who cleans up fifty thousand by rifling the public sits on the jury that throws the book and is considered a leading citizen."

"The gun makes the difference, doesn't it?" said Baranov with a scowl. "Your 'poor slob' can maim or kill. How do you equate that with money?"

"Hold on," I said. "Take your smoothy from behind his desk, put him in the slums, deprive him of any real chance in life, surround him with people with money who don't give a damn for poor slobs and what do you think the smoothy will do? Or, conversely, take the poor slob, clean him, educate him, change his color or heritage if necessary, and put him behind a desk in a cushy job. He won't need any guns, either."

Baranov said, "It's always society according to you bleedingheart—"

For once we had forgotten the existence of Griswold, who, without any assistance from us, actually had his eyes open. His bushy eyebrows curled low and he growled in his deep voice. "What makes you think those two classes of crimes are eternally separate? One can lead to the other. In one case I remember, it did, though I doubt that it would interest you."

He paused to sip at his scotch and soda, and I said, "Even if it didn't interest us, you'd insist on telling us, so go ahead."

The person in question [said Griswold] was named Thomas Appleby and he had a number of qualities, some endearing, some not, all of which collaborated to bring on his violent death.

He was an outgoing person, an extraverted one, a gregarious one. He was short, plump, rubicund, friendly, talkative, unselfconscious. He was what Santa Claus might have looked and acted like, if he had shaved himself clean, cut his hair and gotten into a shirt, jacket and pants.

Appleby had his little vanities. He was an accomplished jokester and could tell his stories with verve and excellence, and being aware of this accomplishment, he practiced it continually and smugly.

He could hold the most unlikely audience enthralled and he rarely failed to get a laugh, usually a big one, from every person in the place. He had an uncommon memory for funny stories; never forgot one; and could continue without repeating, for hours—and sometimes did.

He seemed to pick them up as a mop gathers dust or as a magnet collects pins, and at any given time, he would have a favorite which he would tell as soon as he had a new audience. In fact, he would look for a new audience so he could tell it, and a lot of his gregariousness might have been the result of his steady search for new audiences.

To those who knew him, his favorite story at any time

was called "the Appleby story" and anyone who happened to be trapped when there were a couple of new people in a group might hear it ten times—and even Appleby's appeal faded with repetition.

Another of Appleby's little vanities was that of loving to lean back with an air of importance and beginning a story with "I'm in the government, you know, and I heard this one from a Senator—"

Actually, he was a minor clerk in an obscure branch of HEW, but this particular little vanity hurt no one but himself.

He liked to eat and he managed to consume everything in sight without slowing his ability to talk. He liked his coffee sweet, his asparagus with hollandaise sauce and his pork well done. He avoided liquor and was automatically drawn to any group of strangers, since any group of strangers was a new audience.

All this, of course, and many other facts arose out of the investigation that followed the events of the day of his death. Having gotten out of work a couple of hours early, he walked into a rather dingy coffee shop in one of the lesser hotels of midtown.

It contained a counter in a series of U-shapes and, about one of them, four or five men huddled in ruminative quiet.

Appleby might have found himself a seat at one of the other U's, where there were only two people, widely separated, but he was not interested in empty seats. He headed for the crowd in a straight-line approach.

The story of what then happened came from one of the two people at the other U's, the nearer one, who, it seemed, had a large bump of curiosity, no trouble in hearing Appleby's penetrating voice, and a photographic memory with which to repeat it all.

Appleby slipped into a seat and said cheerfully, "Good afternoon! Good afternoon! Not that it's so good. Damn cold day outside and they're not serving coffee out there and I figure they are in here."

The others looked at him without much friendliness showing, but that meant nothing to Appleby. He did not recognize unfriendliness. He glanced up and down at the menu that he plucked out of its position between a cruet stand and a napkin holder.

He didn't seem to come to an immediate decision. He turned to the person at his right and said, "Heard any good jokes lately?"

The person addressed seemed surprised. Then, with an obvious effort, he said, "No. Nothing much to joke about these days."

Appleby shrugged. "Listen. Jokes don't hurt. They can't make you feel worse, and they might make you feel better."

"Some jokes you hear," said a man who sat hunched over his cigarette and who glowered at Appleby, "make you feel a lot worse."

"Maybe so," said Appleby, "but I work for the government and that makes me an expert on feeling rotten and, I tell you, jokes help. And some of the best jokes I've heard came from strangers. I was once sitting at a counter, like now, and I asked my neighbor for a joke and he handed me a good one. He didn't tell it well—but I can always improve it."

The person at the right took the bait. "What did he tell you?"

"You be the judge," said Appleby, "and tell me if it's a good one. Here it is: Moses came down from Mount Sinai and he had the tables of the law under his arm. He called the elders into conference.

" 'Gentlemen,' he said, 'I have some good news for you and some bad news. The good news is that I was able to hold the boss down to *ten*.' "

Here Appleby, whose voice took on a Charlton Heston quality, but with more authority, when he spoke as Moses, paused to make sure that his listeners allowed smiles to cross their faces.

He then said, " 'But the bad news is that the adultery bit has got to stay.' "

There was an appreciative chuckle and Appleby seemed satisfied to have gotten that much out of an unpromising group. He said to the man behind the counter, "A cup of coffee please, and a cheese Danish." He turned to the man on his left and said, "I shouldn't eat too much, anyway."

"Looks like you already did," said the man on his left with a small snort.

Appleby made it his business to acknowledge hits at himself because it kept his audience in a good mood, which was important. He laughed and said, "You got me. I'm disappointed you noticed. I've been holding my stomach in to make sure you wouldn't."

The coffee made its appearance, and the counterman, as scowling and unfriendly as the men about the counter, said, "Here's cream. You want sugar?"

Appleby had just begun to reach but stared instead at the counterman's open hand, which had within it two little paper packets of sugar.

Appleby hesitated. "Well, why not?" He took one of the packets. "Just one," he said. "I'll try the real thing for once.—Now that's what I call service. Usually, you have to look all over the place for sweeteners and here this guy actually brings it to you. Very thoughtful. Very cooperative. Like Moskowitz's maid. You ever hear the story of Moskowitz, who thought his wife was fooling around?" That, as it turned out, was that month's Appleby story.

"No," said one of the group. "How does it go?"

"Well," said Appleby, "Moskowitz was convinced his wife was fooling around and one day at work he could stand it no more. He had to *know*. So he called home and the maid answered.

" 'Listen,' he said, 'I'm convinced my wife is fooling around, so tell me, is she right now upstairs in the bedroom with another man?'

" 'I must tell you the truth, sir,' said the maid. 'She is. And I must also tell you that I disapprove intensely of such behavior.'

" 'Good,' said Moskowitz. 'I am glad you are a moral person. You know where I keep my gun?'

" 'Yes, sir.'

" 'Then go get it. Take it to my bedroom and shoot that cheating bitch of a wife of mine between the eyes.

Then shoot the man who is violating the sanctity of my home right in the heart. Then return and report to me.' ''

Appleby paused to sip at his coffee. He was holding the audience against their will, he knew. He was in top form, his voice catching every nuance of expression in the conversation of the two characters.

He said "After a pause, the maid was back at the phone. 'Sir,' she said, 'mission accomplished.'

" 'You shot my wife?'

" 'Yes, sir.'

" 'And that no-good deceiving man?'

" 'Yes, sir.'

" 'And they're both dead?'

" 'Yes, sir.'

" 'And what did you do with the gun?'

" 'Sir, I threw it in the swimming pool.'

" 'You threw it in the swimmng pool???—Say, what telephone number is this?' ''

There was a pause of about half a second while the situation sank in, and then there was a simultaneous roar of laughter, which went on for quite a while. The counterman was laughing as hard as the others. Appleby chuckled complacently at his own success, finished his Danish and coffee, and left.

That is the end of the story, except that two hours later, Appleby was found in his apartment, strangled. Nothing was taken. Nothing was damaged. His clothing was disarranged somewhat as though it had been searched, but his wallet was in place, his watch was on his wrist, his ring was on his finger. No known possession was missing.

The police began a routine investigaion, which soon revealed the session in the eating place, which, as it happened, was a haunt of unsavory characters, but nothing had happened which seemed to indicate murder as a possibility. Nor did anything that took place at the coffee shop seem to supply a motive.

It was not a particularly important killing, they thought, and they might have put it on the back burner to simmer, but fortunately, they called me in first. As soon as I heard the story, I thought I could guess what happened as, no doubt, you three can.

"No, we can't," I said in a quiet voice, "and you know we can't. Either you come across or we strangle *you.*"

"Idiots!" muttered Griswold. "Appleby liked his coffee sweet and when the counterman offered him sugar, he said he would take the real thing for a change. That meant he used sugar substitute ordinarily, and it was what he was reaching for at the time. The fact that the counterman offered sugar—a most unusual thing, as Appleby himself pointed out—made it seem as though he were trying to steer his customer away from substitute.

"This instantly brought to my mind the fact that the most common white-collar crime there is—one of which almost everyone is guilty of at one time or another—is helping one's self to those little pink packets of sugar substitute. We've all done it.

"Appleby must have helped himself to several of the pink packets. He would have been stopped ordinarily perhaps, but everyone was laughing at his joke and so no one noticed. Afterward, when they realized the packets were gone, they were certain he had taken them. After all, this stranger was a government man—he had said so himself—and, to all appearances, he had deliberately distracted them so that he could walk off with the packets. They had to be recovered and they were. And he was strangled to keep him from talking."

Baranov said, "How do you guess all this?"

"Because it makes sense. Because it supplies a motive. Suppose that coffee shop served as a place for drug distribution. How innocent to keep heroin in little pink packets that looked exactly like those that hold saccharin. Who would suspect it? Who would give it a second glance? As long as no one gets hold of some by mistake, it was foolproof. And when Appleby walked off with some, it meant panic.

"When the police raided the place, they found I was correct and they made a big haul."

Dollars and Cents

"My own feeling," said Jennings, as we sat in the somewhat brooding and melancholy atmosphere of the Union Club library, "is that in order to cut down on terrorist activity, it would be best to bring down an absolute curtain of silence over it."

"You mean," I said sarcastically, "like not letting anyone know that the President has been shot, in case he's shot."

"No," said Jennings, "that's not what I mean at all. I mean you don't release the name of the would-be assassin, or anything about him, or show any pictures, or talk about him. He becomes a nonperson and so does anyone who's involved in terrorist activity. What's more, you cut down on all television coverage particularly, except for the bare announcement of what is happening."

Baranov said, "I take it you are trying to imply that terrorists do it for the publicity involved. Take away the publicity and there's no point in doing it."

"To a certain extent, yes," said Jennings. "Let's say there's some movement for independence for Fairfield, Connecticut. A Fairfield Liberation Committee is established by five nuts. They call themselves the FLC and begin a campaign of tire slashing in Hartford, sending letters to the newspapers taking credit for it. As the tire slashings continue and as the media give it full exposure, not only does this make the five nuts feel powerful and important, but the publicity actually gets lots of weak-minded people to thinking that there may be something to the notion of making Fairfield independent. On the

113

other hand, if the tire slashings are investigated under cover of a strict news blackout—''

"It just isn't possible," I said, "for two reasons. First, the people whose tires are slashed are going to talk, and rumors will get around that will be worse than the truth. Second, once the principle is established that you can set up a news blackout over something like that, you can do it over anything you conceive as dangerous for people to know, and that means *anything* never in the United States, I hope. Sooner the occasional terrorism.''

"Besides," boomed out Griswold's voice suddenly, "there comes a time when the blackout may break down. How do you keep it secret when you have to evacuate a hotel in the evening rush hour and must send out every fire engine in the area.''

He had both eyes open, the blue of them blazing at us, and he sat erect. It was the widest-awake I'd seen him in years.

"Something you were involved in, Griswold?" I asked.

It began [said Griswold] when a reporter at one of the New York newspapers received a neatly typed, unsigned note, delivered through the mail, to the effect that a dummy bomb had been deposited in a particular room in a particular hotel. The number of the room was given.

The reporter wondered what to do about it, decided it was some sort of gag being pulled on him by one of the jokers about the place, then, after a while, decided he couldn't take the chance. He fished the crumpled letter out of the wastebasket and took it to the police. It meant running the risk of making a fool of himself, but he felt he had no choice.

The police were not in the least sympathetic. They thought it was a gag being pulled on the reporter, too, but *they* had no choice. They sent a member of the bomb squad to the hotel and he was gotten into the room in question. Fortunately, the occupant was not there at the time. Under the eyes of a disapproving hotel official, and feeling very much the jerk, the policeman searched the room rather perfunctorily and, in no time at all, found a box on the shelf in the closet where the extra blankets were stored. On the outside it said in straggly capital letters: BOMB. On the inside was excelsior. Nothing else.

They checked the box for fingerprints, of course. Nothing. The letter was covered by the reporter's fingerprints. It still seemed like a gag of some sort, but more serious than it had been considered at first. The reporter was instructed to bring any further letter to the police forthwith and to try not to handle it. He took to opening his letters while wearing kid gloves.

It turned out to be a useful precaution, because three days later he received another letter. It named another hotel and gave the room number again. He brought it in at once and a member of the bomb squad was sent out. A box filled with bits of cardboard was found in the bathroom, wedged behind the toilet seat. It also said: BOMB.

No fingerprints anywhere.

The police had informed all the general newspapers of the city of what had happened, had asked for no publicity to avert panic, and had urged them all to watch for the letters.

A good thing, too, for the third letter came to a different reporter on a different paper. Same as the others except that this time there was an additional paragraph, which said, "I trust you understand all this is practice. One of these days, it will be the real thing. In that case, of course, I will not give you the room number."

By that time, the police called me in and showed me the letters.

I said, "What has the lab found out?"

My friend on the force, a police lieutenant named Cassidy, said, "It's an electric typewriter, undoubtedly an IBM product, and the fake bomber is a man of education and an accomplished typist. No fingerprints. Nothing distinctive about either paper or envelope, or about the fake bombs for that matter. The postmark indicates the letters were posted from different places, but all in Manhattan."

"That doesn't seem particularly helpful."

Cassidy curled his lip. "It sure doesn't. Do you know how many IBM elcctric typewriters there are in Manhattan? And how many good typists with some education there are? If he sends enough letters, though, we'll be able to gather more information, I hope."

I could see nothing further to do, either. I may be extraordinarily good at understanding the trifles that escape others, uncanny even—but it is only everyone else who considers me a miracle man. I make no such claims on my own behalf. Still, I stayed in close touch for the duration of the case.

Additional letters did come and they did contain more information, at least as to motive. The mysterious bomber began to express himself more freely. He was apparently sick and tired of our money-mad society and wanted a return to a purer, more spiritual day. Just how this would be effected by his antics, he didn't say.

I said to Cassidy, "He clearly doesn't have any trouble getting into hotel rooms, but then there's no reason why he should."

"Oh," said Cassidy, "skeleton keys?"

"Simpler," I said. "Every room is cleaned every day. The cleaning women occasionally wander off on some errand while cleaning and leave doors open, especially if the room is between occupants and there are no personal items in it to be stolen. In fact, I have seen hotelroom doors open and cleaning women nowhere in sight, even when there is luggage and clothing in clear view. No one stops anyone from wandering about hotel corridors so all our bomber has to do is to find an open door."

The word went out to every hotel in New York that cleaning women were on no account to leave room doors open. Some of the hotels instructed the women to keep an eye out for small boxes and to call anything that seemed suspicious to the attention of the management.

One box turned up and reached police headquarters before the letter announcing it arrived. The letter was delayed in the mail, which is not really surprising.

"I hope," said Cassidy dolefully, "that when it's the

real thing, he doesn't announce it by mail. It will never come in time to give us a chance."

The precautions about leaving doors open slowed up the bomber. The letters were fewer, but they didn't stop altogether. Increasing difficulty seemed to make him more irritable. He denounced the banks and financiers generally. The police psychologists tried to work up a personality profile of the letter writer from what he said. Banks were asked whether anyone had been refused a loan who had reacted to that refusal with unusual bitterness or with threats. Continued analysis of the postmarks on the letters seemed to pinpoint some neighborhoods in preference to others as the bomber's home ground.

Cassidy said, "If he keeps it up long enough, we'll get him."

"But one of these days," I said, "it will be the real thing and very likely before we've managed to squeeze him out of the several million who live or work in Manhattan."

"This may go on quite awhile, though. He may be in no position to make or get a bomb. All this fake-bomb stuff is a way of blowing off steam and when he's blown off enough, he'll stop."

"That would be nice," I said, "but these days I imagine anyone can manage to get an explosive device or learn to make one, if he tries long enough."

And then one day, a police officer came hurriedly to Cassidy. He said, "A guy claiming to be the fake bomber was on the phone."

Cassidy started to his feet, but the officer said, "He's off the phone. We couldn't hold him. He says he'll call again.—And he says it's the real thing, now."

He called a half-dozen times, at intervals, from different public coin telephones. The bomb, he said, was placed. The *real* bomb. He named the hotel—only the newest in Manhattan. And he named the time for which it was set: 5 P.M. that day—only the peak of the rush hour.

"You have time to evacuate the hotel," he said in a hoarse whisper. "I don't want anyone to die. I just want to strike at property to teach a lesson to those who place property before humanity."

It was a little after 2 P.M. when he finally gave us the place and time. There was time to do the job, but considering not only the evacuation, but the cordoning-off of the area, and the gathering of fire engines, there would be an incredible tie-up of Manhattan traffic.

Cassidy, on the phone, did his best. "Look," he said in as ingratiating a manner as he could manage. "You're an idealist. You're a man of honor. You want no one hurt. Suppose we don't manage to get everyone out. Suppose we leave a child behind despite all we can do. Would you want that on your conscience? Just let us have the room number. Do that and I will guarantee you a fair hearing on your grievances."

The bomber wasn't buying that. He said, "I'll call back."

Fifteen interminable minutes later, during which the police and the bomb squad were making for the spot, we got the call.

"All right," he said. "Dollars and cents. That's all people think about. Dollars and cents. If you're too dumb to understand that, then I'm not responsible. *You* are." He hung up.

Cassidy stared at the dead phone. "What the devil did he mean by that?"

But I had heard the conversation on the conference-call tie-in and said urgently, "Hold off on the evacuation just a few minutes. The bomb squad is on the scene by now. Get in touch with them. I think I've got the room number, and they may be able to handle the bomb on the spot."

I was right. The bomb, a simple but real one, was easily dismantled without disturbing anyone in the hotel. We didn't get the bomber, but he's never tried again. He'd apparently had enough, and since no one was hurt—

Griswold's words trailed off into a soft snore, and Jennings called out, "Don't go to sleep, damn it. Where did you get the room number from? What was the clue?"

I followed my usual practice of stamping on Griswold's nearer foot, but he was prepared for me this time and kicked my ankle rather sharply.

He said, "I *told* you the clue. The bomber said 'dollars and cents' and said if we were too dumb to understand that, *we* were responsible."

"That's a *clue?*" said Baranov. "That's just his standard complaint about the money-mad society."

"It could be that, too, but I felt it to be the clue. I told you the man was an expert typist, and a typist tends to think of words in terms of typewriter keys."

I said, "I'm an expert typist, and the phrase means nothing to me."

"I'm not surprised about that," said Griswold rather nastily. "But if you type 'dollars and cents,' and are pressed for time, you are quite likely to type the symbols '$&c' " and he made the signs in the air.

"You can do that by tapping three typewriter keys on the IBM electrics with the shift key depressed. If you *don't* depress the shift key, those same keys give you the number 476. Try it and see. So I thought we might gamble on Room 476, and that was it."

Friends and Allies

"Did you watch the wedding of Prince Charles and Lady Diana?" I asked, with my legs stretched out in comfort, something the atmosphere of the Union library didn't ordinarily encourage.

"Yes," said Jennings enthusiastically. "What a fairy-tale princess! Young! Blond! Beautiful!"

"And at the same time," I said, "Britain's cities are torn by riots. Northern Ireland is aflame. Inflation and unemployment are both unbearably high."

"All the more reason," said Baranov with a touch of antagonism in his voice, "for the spectacle. The British gathered in hordes to watch. If the Royal Family had said the marriage would take place at City Hall and the money saved would be donated to the poor, there would have been a fire storm of protest."

I sighed. "You're probably right. The human race has an enormous irrationality about it; or perhaps it's just the British."

Jennings said, "Listen! Back in 1940, we were delighted that the British were irrational. Every rational consideration would have said: give up and make a compromise peace with Hitler. Instead, they let London burn, and risked total destruction and enslavement."

Well, there was nothing to say to that. I just nodded.

"And," Jennings said, pursuing his advantage, "they're our friends and allies."

I nodded again.

Griswold took this moment to open the blue icicles he called his eyes and gazed at us bleakly. He cleared his

120

throat, brought his scotch and soda to his lips and said, "There are no such things as friends and allies. Just temporary accommodations.

"You mean the British—" began Jennings hotly.

"I mean they have their interests," said Griswold, "and we have ours, and though they might run on parallel paths, those paths are never quite identical. For that matter, there are no such things as enemies and opponents. Just temporary divergences."

"That is *so* cynical," said Baranov.

The truth [said Griswold] sounds cynical so often that people prefer to believe lies. That's the source of much of the trouble in the world. I remember a time, back in 1956, when the Cold War was at its height and the Soviet Union was experiencing revolts in Eastern Europe. We were reasonably concerned, at that time, to keep the whole thing as mild as possible and avoid a nuclear showdown—in other words, to weaken the Soviet Union, but not to drive them insane.

So were the British, but they were afraid *we* might react with a touch of insanity, and we were concerned lest their fears weaken the united front of Western resolution.

This created difficulties for us. The British and we each have our own intelligence operations. The two are completely independent. Because the British are our friends and allies, we tell them everything we know— provided we feel they ought to know it. And the same is true the other way around.

The trouble is that they always feel they should know *everything* we know, and we don't think so at all. And that's true the other way around, too.

You see the tangle.

John Foster Dulles was Secretary of State at the time and he believed in brinkmanship and eyeballing, and that made the British nervous. What they desperately didn't want to do was to give him any ammunition that would send him flying off the handle. Then, too, Great Britain had plans of its own for the Middle East at the time, plans they didn't want us to know.

On the other hand, the professionals in the State Department always took the position that Dulles was most unpredictable and therefore most dangerous when he didn't have the facts and had to guess, for he tended to guess a worst-case scenario.

So among other ways of gathering information, we managed to infiltrate British intelligence. We knew the Soviets had probably done so, and why shouldn't we? No doubt the British tried to infiltrate our intelligence and had, perhaps, succeeded.

Infiltrating the British was a super-delicate job. The British expected the Soviets to attempt the job and they accepted that fact philosophically and harbored no ill feelings. They wouldn't accept the same from us, however. *We* were friends and allies. So we had to work a lot harder to keep the British unsuspecting than ever the Soviets had to.

In any case, the information reached our people in a very roundabout way. It was just a date—June 8. It doesn't matter what it meant exactly, and I won't tell you, because even *today* it would be improper to do so. Too many secrets are involved that are still secrets.

However, the British were going to do something on June 8, and when they did, it would give us a handle for our proper response to Soviet action in Eastern Europe. If the British action had remained unknown to us, we would have been reacting to the Soviets with key information missing.

I'm sorry if this all sounds complicated, but nothing is straightforward in the labyrinth of spy and counterspy.

Anyway, we thought we had the date. We made preparations in the more or less secure knowledge that we knew what was on the minds of the people in London, and on June 8, what we were sure would happen didn't happen!

Did that mean that the British had changed their plan? Or did it mean that our leak in the British Intelligence had been plugged and that false information had been deliberately fed us to teach us a lesson?

Or that someone had simply made a mistake?

A few days passed with tension rising in Washington

till you could feel it vibrate in the air. Everyone in our own Intelligence was wondering how long it could all be kept from Dulles.

Finally, they called me in. They usually get to me when they run out of everything else.

I would rather have stayed out. I felt Dulles's policy in the Middle East was disastrous, and I had been given my walking papers—for the fifteenth time, I think—because I said so openly. An old friend of mine, however, called me in, so I had to oblige him.

That's always been my weakness. Soft as butter. Besides, it was clear to me that the Middle East would soon boil over with incalculable consequences, so I had to help out.

My old friend—I'll call him Jim, just to give him a handle—explained the situation to me, without giving me any of the real details. Dulles would have been furious if he had found out I had been made privy to anything really delicate, and Jim had to keep that in mind.

I said, "It seems to me then, Jim, that you've got a date and it's the wrong date. How the devil can I help you?"

"Well," said Jim, who was sweating profusely, "I'm convinced our man in London is still in the clear, and the British aren't showing any of the excitement you would expect if they had done anything like switching dates, or misleading us on purpose. My feeling is that, somehow, someone has made a mistake. We have ended up with the wrong date and the right date is still out there somewhere."

I said, "All right, get to your man in London and ask him to give you the date again."

"We can't," said Jim. "He's out of reach right now. The British have just given him an assignment he couldn't duck.—After all, he *is* an Englishman, even if he does work for us. We don't know where he is, and since he doesn't know we're in a jam, there's no reason for him to be trying to reach us."

"I still don't see what I can do. Do you have the date clear? Or in code?"

"Clear. J-U-N-E-8. No chance of a coding—or decoding—mistake."

"How did your man in London deliver it?"

"Quite indirectly, but surely. He fished the last cigarette out of a pack and tossed the empty pack into a wastebasket. A little while later, a poorly dressed man scrabbled for a newspaper in the wastebasket and pulled out the cigarette pack with it. Inside the pack was the date—written with a special pen that had a small nib bent at right angles."

"The 'poorly dressed man' was, I presume, one of ours."

"Yes, he burnt the cigarette pack, recorded the date and passed it along in a totally different way. Nothing could be traced to our first man, whose position had to be protected, and the second man was dispensable—as he well knew."

"You think the second man made a mistake in copying the date?"

"We've used him before. He's never made a mistake. —Yes, yes, I know. Always a first time. He swears he made no mistake. June 8, absolutely. No way of having mistaken it. He insists on that."

"In that case, your first man—your man in London—must have gotten the wrong date and you're out of luck. Unless the British *did* do whatever they're supposed to have done on June 8, but did it so quietly that you never noticed."

"Impossible. If you knew what it was, you wouldn't think that."

"What about the second man? No matter how well he has done for you in the past, if he's just a London ragpicker you've hired, someone else can outbid you and 'un-hire' him, so to speak."

"London ragpicker?" said Jim indignantly. "He was born in Dallas. Graduate of Texas A & M. One of our best."

"Ah! The light, just possibly, dawns."

"Where?"

"Never mind," I said austerely. After all, if he felt it

was all right to withhold information from me, I saw no reason why I couldn't return the compliment.

"Suppose I give you an alternate date. Can you hold the fort and keep us from charging blindly forward till then?"

"What alternate date?"

I told him.

He frowned. "What makes you think that's the alternate date?"

I fixed him with my frank and honest glance. "Have you ever known me to be wrong, when I have said I'm right?"

"Well, as a matter of fact——"

"Don't be a wise guy. Just hold the fort—and keep me out of it. If Dulles finds out I had something to do with this, he would rather risk nuclear war than be safe on my say-so."

He said, "Well, I'll try."

He succeeded. Revolts in both Poland and Hungary were crushed that year, but the United States took the kind of action that kept the Soviets on the griddle. The point was that they were *not* able to intervene in the Middle East, when Britain, France and Israel attacked Egypt later that year, and that was more important. Most important of all, there was no nuclear war.

So don't tell *me* "friends and allies."

"Do you propose to leave it there?" I asked.

"Why not?" said Griswold. "It's a happy ending, isn't it?"

"Sure, but what was the alternate date, and how did you get it?"

Griswold puffed out his breath and his white mustache flew in the air before it. He shook his head.

"Look," he said. "Our man in London wrote the date inside the cigarette pack; far inside, one would suspect, to make it the less noticeable to casual inspection. Operating a bent pen and making the writing clear is a delicate job, and he wasn't going to write an encyclopedia. I was sure he would write the date as concisely as possible, meaning that he wrote it '6/8.' Wouldn't you say so?"

"Reasonable," said Jennings.

"And the second man, our Texan, sending it on in a different way, could afford to be more lavish and scrawled a 'June 8' on something and sent it along in whatever hidden fashion was used."

"So what?" said Baranov.

"Well, don't you think there's a question as to which number represented the month and which the day? In the United States, we tend to let the first number represent the month, but in Great Britain, they tend to let the second number represent the month. The second man, an American, seeing 6/8, writes it down as June 8, June being the sixth month. He never gives the matter a second thought, and swears that is what he saw. But our British man in London was symbolizing '6 August,' August being the eighth month, so that was my alternate date. August 6. A very good date and, as it turned out, the correct one."

Which Is Which?

I was feeling grumpy. I knew it wouldn't last. I had a pleasant sherry in my hand, a comfortable chair under me, the dowdy but quiet atmosphere of the Union Club library about me, and Griswold—a somnolent figure in his personal armchair—across the way.

Still, I wanted to use the grumpiness while it lasted. I said, "I wish I knew how to make a citizen's arrest. I know it exists, but I have never heard of it actually being done."

"Whom do you want to arrest?" asked Jennings lazily. "Griswold?"

I snorted, "Why arrest Griswold? He's a symphony of arrested motion as it is. No, the people I want to arrest are the smokers in elevators. They are clear law-breakers and I want to be able to pull out my handcuffs—"

Baranov said with interest, "Handcuffs? You carry handcuffs?"

"I was speaking symbolically, for Heaven's sake. I put my hand on the person's shoulder—"

Jennings said, "In the first place, if you do that, he will punch you in the face, if he's a he, or kick you in the shins, if she's a she. And if for any reason somebody should submit to your citizen's arrest, what will you do? Take them to the nearest police station? Do you know where it is? And if you're in an elevator, you're probably going somewhere. Do you abandon that and just become an off-duty policeman? Do you—"

"Oh, shut up," I said, suddenly more grumpy than ever.

Whereupon Griswold stirred, brought his scotch and soda to his lips, took a careful sip and said, "I once made a citizen's arrest. A policeman was on the scene, as it happened, but he was in no position to make the arrest."

I turned on him savagely. "And *you* were? Just how do you explain that?"

"No way at all—unless you ask me to do so politely."

But I knew I wouldn't have to.

Their names were Moe and Joe [said Griswold] and I don't know that anyone in the course of their criminal career ever called them anything else. They must have had last names, but those were never used, except in court, and I don't remember what they were.

The surprising thing about them was that they were not twins. In fact, Moe was Jewish and Joe was an Italian Catholic, but through some peculiar twist of the genes, they looked enormously similar. They could have said they were twins and they would have been believed. In fact, I suspect that many who knew them thought they *were* twins.

They met in high school, which neither of them finished, and discovered their similarity then. Moe had just moved into the neighborhood and was two months older than Joe. Both were fascinated by the similarity and they used it in horseplay. One would borrow a quarter and when asked for repayment would insist it had been the other who had done the borrowing. The other, of course, denied it. In the end they paid up, since otherwise the sources of credit would have dried up. But this, and a few other little tricks of the sort, undoubtedly gave them the notion for what was to become their lifelong career.

They became close friends and cultivated a similarity in clothes, speech, and characteristic ways when they were old enough to rid themselves of unnecessary family ties. They roomed together and were sufficiently close in size to be able to share a wardrobe. They took to wearing identical styles and colors, and, except when taking a vacation from each other, made sure that they wore brother-and-brother outfits.

They also made sure that they were not often seen

together except in their special haunts and by their special boon companions.

Little by little, they developed their separate specialties. Moe was a clever con-man, who could always manage to wheedle a few bills out of some innocent. Joe was a nimble pickpocket, who could lift those same bills with equal celerity.

They were careful never to undertake a large job. They merely nickel-and-dimed it in order to be fairly well-off without having to work. I suppose that the small element of danger was exhilarating.

Just the same, they were not *that* enamored of danger, for they took care to minimize the risk, and that was where the twinship came in. If one was attempting a job of more-than-average magnitude, the other would set up an alibi.

Let Joe, for instance, break into an apartment, and that night Moe would be playing poker with half a dozen people of unimpeachable honesty and he would be playing honestly, too. *If* Joe were seen at the scene of the crime, and the police came about to investigate, he would come out with Moe's alibi—the names of the people, the hands he had held, and so on. Naturally, he would have been fed all the information by Moe, and the other poker players would have no choice but to uphold Joe. Even if Joe and Moe were presented to them in the lineup, they could not have sworn to one rather than the other—not without being ripped apart in cross-examination.

The very few occasions in which the police got the idea that the two of them were working in combination, they saw no way of getting witnesses to distinguish between them, and had to be content with warning them and making threatening noises—which the two ignored.

Moe and Joe even got to the point where they occasionally joked about it. Moe would casually help himself to a couple of apples from a fruit stand and walk to the corner. The proprietor, stunned for a moment by the effrontery of it, would finally come to himself and set out in chase, shouting names. Moe would have turned the corner and when the proprietor also turned, he would find Moe standing with Joe, and each grinning and pointing to the other.

By being moderate in their goals, Moe and Joe managed to gain a minor prosperity without arousing too much official frustration or public outcry, and the prosperity showed in their attire. They took to wearing string ties of interesting and identical design, and, since both were nearsighted, both adopted black-rimmed glasses with the kind of lenses that darkened after a minute or so in the sunlight and then cleared after a minute or so indoors. They had their hair styled by the same barber, and each carried the same kind of umbrella at any hint of rain.

This is not to say they couldn't be told apart. Moe was half an inch taller than Joe. Their dental work was different, and they had different eyeglass prescriptions. Joe had a small scar under one ear and Moe's eyebrows were bushier. These were not the sorts of things, however, that the casual witness could swear to with any certainty, or even credibility.

I suppose they might have gone on forever, if it weren't for one bad break—but then bad breaks are bound to come if you take risks long enough. Even small risks.

Joe had cased a small jewelry shop and it seemed to him that if he came in during lunch hour when the place was crowded, he would be able to ask to be shown a case of rings and could manage to palm one of them, and substitute a piece of fine glass. Just in case something went wrong, he had stationed Moe in a nearby hotel lobby.

Well, something went wrong. Even the finest prestidigitator can get an attack of the dropsy now and then, and Joe, receiving an accidental nudge from the person next to him at just the wrong time, dropped the ring. The proprietor of the store noted the event, drew the correct conclusion at once, and, being an irascible man who had been burglarized in the past and was tired of it, drew a gun.

Customers scattered, and Joe, who was not a man of violence, panicked. He tried to grab the gun to keep it from being fired in his direction. There was a short struggle, and the gun went off.

As happens too often in such cases, the bullet was stopped by the honest citizen. The jeweler dropped, and if Joe had panicked before, he was in a frenzy now. He dashed out of the store, intent on making it to the hotel lobby, picking up Moe, and then clearing out of town for a good long time.

But once bad breaks start coming, they don't stop easily. These days you hardly ever see a policeman in the street, but there was one outside the jewelry store. He heard the shot, he saw a man running and he took off in pursuit.

And then, of course, we have to add one topper to the thing, the cherry on top of the sundae. I was in the street, too. When you stop to think of it, having Joe get himself into such a mess and having not only a policeman but me waiting for him—each of us there for two thoroughly independent reasons—is asking too much of coincidence. Just the same, it can happen, and on this occasion it did.

It was a bright, sunny day, not a cloud in the sky, cool and dry, so the avenue was as crowded as it is ever likely to get. This meant it might be easy to lose Joe, but it also meant he couldn't get on much speed. He had to twist and turn and he was wearing a checked summer jacket, in shades of blue, that made him stand out.

The policeman, as it happened, had heard the shot and had seen Joe come flying out of the jewelry shop and would have run after him even if he hadn't known him—but he did. Joe was a familiar figure to him.

Of course, with the street crowded, the policeman couldn't threaten to shoot; he couldn't go near his gun. He might have expected someone in the crowd to tackle Joe, if he were out of touch with reality. Naturally, no one did. The crowd scattered, following the unwritten law of today, "Thou shalt not get involved!"

The policeman wasn't going to have much chance if the pursuit was a long and involved one, for he was out of condition, and to tell you the truth I was going to do even worse. It wasn't many years ago that this happened, and I was already past those days when I was young and lissome. I managed a fast trot, which was clearly going to get me in third in a field of three.

Fortunately for us, if not for Joe, Joe didn't keep up the race. He had no chance for thought and only knew he had to run to the safety of Moe. He ducked into the hotel not more than a block and a half from the scene of the crime. Ten seconds afterward, the policeman ran through the entrance, and fifteen seconds after that, I ran in.

Joe was standing right there, and Moe was next to him. Both were in blue-checked jackets, darker-blue trousers, black belts, string ties, and Moe was putting on the show of his life. His hair was mussed up, as Joe's was, and he was panting. He even looked a little moist, perhaps from anxiety, as Joe was, from running.

By God, Joe even managed a grin, pointed at Moe, and said, "This guy just ran in here."

And Moe managed the same grin, pointed at Joe and said, "No, he did."

The policeman glared from one to the other and shouted, "Did anyone here notice which one of these jokers just ran into the lobby?"

He might just as well have asked if anyone knew the middle name of his Aunt Jemima.

But I had caught my breath by this time and I put my hand firmly on Joe's shoulder and said, "Officer, this is the man, and I am making a citizen's arrest until you can manage the real thing."

He didn't know me. "What makes *you* so sure?" he asked.

"See for yourself," I said. "And what's more, his pal, or his twin, or whatever is going to back us up, because this wasn't just a robbery. A shot was fired, my friend," I said to Moe, whose name and background I didn't know at this time, "and it's certainly assault, and very likely murder during the commission of a felony. Are you sure you want to be an accessory after the fact in a thing like that?"

Moe cast a horrified glance at Joe, and it was clear he didn't.

We had no trouble. The jeweler was only wounded, but Joe got a sentence that put him away for a while and Moe had a lesson he wouldn't forget either.

Griswold had that rotten air of satisfaction he always gets when he tells of one of his triumphs, and Baranov said, "And how did you know which one of the two had just run into the lobby?"

"Yes," said Jennings, "and in a way that would stick in court."

"No problem at all," said Griswold with a distinct sneer. "I told you they both wore glasses of the kind that darken in the sunlight and clear again indoors, and I told you it was a bright, sunny day. One of those two had just run in from the sunlight, and his glasses were still dark, while the other's glasses were not. I pointed that out to the policeman before Joe's glasses had quite cleared, and Moe, seeing we had his pal cold, was quite willing to testify against him to save his own neck."

The Sign

Baranov said, "According to the forecast in the daily paper, today was a good day for taking financial risks, so I bet a friend of mine fifty cents it wouldn't rain this afternoon and you saw what happened. It poured! The question is: should I sue the forecaster?"

I said with infinite disdain (for I had carefully carried an umbrella), "By forecast, I presume you mean the astrological column?"

"Do you suppose I meant the weather forecast?" said Baranov tartly. "Of course I meant the astrologer. Who else would tell me to take financial risks?"

"The weatherman," said Jennings, "said 'partly cloudy.' He didn't predict rain, either."

I refused to be lured off the track. "Asking a stupid question isn't as bad as falling for stupid mysticism. Since when has astrology impressed you as a substitute for financial acumen?"

"Reading the column is an amusement," said Baranov stiffly, "and I can afford fifty cents."

"The question is whether you can afford intellectual decay. I think not," I said.

In his high-backed armchair in the library of the Union Club where we all sat, Griswold was comfortably asleep to the tune of a faint snoring. But now he attracted our attention when he scraped the sole of his shoe on the floor, as he shifted position without spilling the drink he held in his hand.

I said softly, "You know the way he's always reminded of a story by anything we say. I'll bet if we wake him up and talk about astrology, he won't be able to think of a thing."

Baranov said eagerly, "I'll take that bet. Fifty cents. I want to make it back."

At this point, Griswold's drink moved toward his lips. He sipped daintily, his eyes still closed. He said, "As it happens, I do have an astrological story to tell, so hand over the half-dollar."

The last was addressed to me, and Griswold opened his eyes now to reinforce the remark.

I said, "You'll have to tell the story first."

The most delicate job a spy can have [said Griswold] is recruiting. How do you persuade someone else to betray his country without revealing your own position?

For that matter, the problem is a difficult one for the person being recruited. There have been cases of perfectly loyal government employees—whether civilian or armed service—who allowed recruiting efforts to go on because they honestly didn't understand what was happening, or because they thought the other fellow was joking.

By the time they do report—if they do—there may be people in government intelligence who have grown suspicious of them, and their careers may therefore be inhibited or ruined without their having ever really done anything out of the way.

In fact, I have known cases where the recruiting agent deliberately spread suspicion against his victim in order to enrage the poor person against the government for falsely suspecting him. The person in question is then actually recruited.

The man I am going to tell you about, whom I shall refer to as Davis, avoided the obvious pitfalls.

He carefully reported the first sign of recruitment to his superior, whom we shall call Lindstrom, at a time when, in fact, what had occurred might well have been only idle conversation. It was, however, during those years when Senator McCarthy had inflamed American public opinion and had reduced men in public office to near hysteria.

Davis was, however, a man of integrity. Though he reported the incident, he refused to give the name of the army officer who was involved. His reasoning was that it might indeed have been an innocent conversation and that, in the heat of the times, his testimony could serve to destroy a man unjustly.

That put Lindstrom in a delicate position. He himself might be victimized if things went wrong. Nevertheless, he was a man of integrity too, so he accepted Davis's reserve, assured him he would bear witness to his loyalty in reporting, and in writing (carefully worded, you may be sure) ordered him to play along until he was certain that the person involved was really disloyal and then to give his name.

Davis was worth recruiting, you understand. It was before the days when computers became omnipresent, and Davis was one of the very few who had his finger on the statistical records of the government. He knew where all the dossiers were, and he had access to them. He could conjure up more rapidly than one would believe possible, considering that he had no computer to help him, the intimate details of any one of millions of people.

It would make, of course, an unparalleled instrument for blackmail, if Davis could be persuaded in that direction, but Davis—a single man who could afford to be single-minded—had thought for only one thing, his hobby.

He was an astrologer. No, not the kind you think. He didn't prepare horoscopes or make predictions. He had a strictly scientific interest. He was trying to see whether, in truth, one could correlate the signs of the zodiac with personal characteristics or with events. He was studying all the people in Leo, all the people in Capricorn and so on, and trying to find out if a disproportionate number of Leos were athletes, or whether Capricornians were prone to be scientists and so on.

I don't think he ever found out anything useful, but it was his obsession. In his department, the standing joke was that he might not know someone's name, but he surely knew his sign.

Eventually, he was convinced that the recruitment

was seriously meant, and he grew increasingly indignant. He told Lindstrom that the traitor would be coming to his apartment to work out the final details, and that he (Davis) would come to Lindstrom at midnight with the full details.

But Davis was not an experienced operator. The recruiter had divined the fact that Davis might be reporting to the authorities and took the most direct action to stop him.

When Davis didn't keep his midnight appointment, Lindstrom went to Davis's apartment and found him there—knifed.

He did not find him quite dead, however. Davis's eyes opened and he stared glassily at Lindstrom. Davis was lying across a small table and trying feebly to reach toward some file cards resting nearby. There were four of them, all somewhat bloodstained.

Davis mumbled, "Should have known—misfit—only sign doesn't fit the name." Then he died.

The next day, at noon, I got a phone call from Lindstrom, begging me to come see him at once! I was reluctant to do so because it would mean missing the first game of the World Series on my brand-new television set, but Lindstrom grew so panicky I had no choice.

When I arrived, Lindstrom was in conference with a young first lieutenant, who looked even more dreadfully disturbed than Lindstrom did. The entire department must have been in turmoil that day. As soon as I came, though, Lindstrom sent the lieutenant away, saying absently after him, "And happy birthday."

He waited till the lieutenant was gone, then opened the door, made sure the corridor was empty and returned.

I said sardonically, "Are you sure this place isn't bugged?"

"I've checked it," he said quite seriously. Then he told me what had happened.

"Too bad," I said.

"Worse than that," he said. "Here's a man who knew of a traitor right in our department and I didn't force the information out of him at once. Now I've lost the man, *and* the traitor and McCarthy will have my head for it."

"Will he find out?" I asked.

"Of course. There must be at least one person in this department who reports to him regularly."

"Do you have any leads?"

"Not really. The four cards on the table were Davis's own cards, the kind he uses to file and cross-file human characteristics against astrological signs.—That's his obsession. Let me explain!" And he did.

I said, "What were the four cards doing there?"

"Perhaps nothing. They were four officers in this department, and I don't know what he was doing with them. Still, he was reaching toward them as though he wanted to take one or point to one and he talked about someone being a misfit, with a sign that didn't fit his name."

"He didn't say his name?"

"No. He was dying, almost dead. His last thought was of his obsession: his damned astrological signs."

"Then you don't know which of the four it is."

"That's right. And as long as we don't know, all four will be under suspicion. That will mean ruined careers if McCarthy zeroes in on it; and for at least three of them, possibly all four, it would be an incredible injustice. Listen, do you know the astrological signs?"

"Yes, certainly. Aries the Ram, Taurus the Bull, Gemini the Twins, Cancer the Crab, Leo the Lion, Virgo the Virgin, Libra the Scales, Scorpio the Scorpion, Sagittarius the Archer, Capricorn the Goat, Aquarius the Water Bearer and Pisces the Fish. Twelve of them, in that order. Aries governs the month beginning March 21, and the rest follow, month by month."

"All right," said Lindstrom, "and the English names are all direct translations of the Latin. I checked that. So Davis's remark about the sign not fitting the name doesn't refer to that. The only alternative is that the name of the sign doesn't fit the name of the officer. The cards had each the name of an officer and, among other personal data, the sign he was born under."

"Any obvious misfits?"

"No, the four names happen, by a miserable chance, to be utterly common; Joseph Brown, John Jones, Thomas

Smith and William Clark; and not one of the names, first, last, or in combination, seems to either fit, or not fit, the person's sign in any way."

"Does each have a different sign?"

"Yes."

"And what do you want me to do?"

Lindstrom looked at me out of a face twisted in misery. "Help me. I have the cards. They've been checked for fingerprints and only Davis's have been found. Look them over and see if you can see anything in them that will make sense to you in the light of Davis's final remark."

I said, "I may have the answer now. That first lieutenant who was here when I came in—You wouldn't talk until you were sure he was gone. You even looked out in the hall to make sure he wasn't hanging about near the door. Was his one of the names on the list?"

"Yes, as a matter of fact. He's Lieutenant Tom Smith."

"Then I think he's your man. Judging by his face, he was in a bad way. Call him in, with a witness, and tackle him hard, and I'm sure he'll break."

He *did* break. We had the traitor; and three innocent men (four, counting Lindstrom) were saved.

Griswold looked smug and self-satisfied, and I said, "Griswold, you've made that up. There's no way you could have gotten the answer on the information you had."

Griswold looked at me haughtily. "No way *you* could have. I said I was called in the first day of the World Series. That meant early October. Count the astrological signs from Aries, which governs the month beginning March 21, and you'll find that six months afterward comes Libra, which governs the month beginning September 22. Lindstrom wished the lieutenant a happy birthday, so he was born in early October under the sign of Libra."

"So?" I said with a sarcastic inflection.

"So Davis said 'the sign doesn't fit *the* name,' not '*his* name.' It wasn't the *man's* name being referred to. The signs are all part of the zodiac and, in Greek, 'zodiac'

means 'circle of animals.' You don't have to know Greek
to see that the beginning 'zo' is in 'zoo' and 'zoology.'
Well, look at the list of signs: ram, bull, crab, lion,
scorpion, goat and fish—seven animals. If you remember
that human beings are part of the animal kingdom, there
are four more: a pair of twins, a virgin, an archer, and a
water bearer. Eleven animals altogether. One and only
one sign is not an animal, or even alive. It is the *only*
sign that doesn't fit the name of zodiac. Since the four
names were all officers in the department and I met one
officer, who looked miserable and who was a Libra, I
thought that *if* he was one of the four, he was also the
supposed misfit, and the murderer. Well, he *was* one of
the four, and he *was* the murderer."

So I paid Baranov the half-dollar, and the bum took it.

Catching the Fox

"Drugs," said Jennings thoughtfully, "are strictly a twentieth-century problem, I think. All through history people have been chewing on plants to get hashish or cocaine or nicotine or anything that would make them feel good in a lousy world. No one worried about addiction, physical harm, lowered life expectancy. Life expectancy was only thirty-five or less anyway."

"I know," said Baranov. "I think sometimes—if they want it, let them have it. No one ever mugged someone because he *had* his shot; only because he didn't, and needed money to buy one. I don't want to give up my life just to keep someone from having his shot; sooner his life than mine."

I had difficulty respecting the quiet of the Union Club library, but I managed to keep my voice under control. "You two cementheads talk that way because you feel that drugs are just a matter of bums, college weirdos and ghetto people. You can't isolate it like that. Once you have a drug-ridden society, we're all potential victims— you, me, and our kids. Then, too, we have worse drugs now than any that plant life has ever manufactured, thanks to our clever chemists."

"Larry Liberal is heard from," said Baranov, lifting a lip. "Everything is either society's fault or society's responsibility. Even if we try to stop it, we always fail. So?"

"Then we fail; but we've still got to *try*," I said earnestly. "If we quit, if we let it take over unopposed—"

From the depths of Griswold's armchair came his

deep voice. "Have you been fighting drugs, or just talking."

"Have *you* been fighting it?" I asked hostilely.

Griswold said, "Once or twice."

"Oh?" said Jennings. "Have you been on an anti-drug detail?"

"No! But I've been consulted by those who have been. I was frequently consulted on all sorts of things. Drugs too, of course. Naturally, I don't suppose you are interested."

I said, "We'll pretend we're interested, Griswold. Go ahead."

The trouble with grand theories of crime [said Griswold] is that they don't help the law-enforcement officer.

A policeman, a treasury agent, a secret-service man can't do his job by considering the effect of societal reform, or psychiatric expertise. Invariably, he is facing some specific criminal event, some particular crime and criminal; and he must come up with something specific in response.

Everything sometimes works its way down to a single cat-and-mouse game—with nothing else counting.

This was the case with Lieutenant Hoskins (not his real name, of course) on a particular police force, who was faced with the drug problem in his particular city.

It began in a broad, general way, with newspapers pointing up the enormousness of the problem, and speaking of the degeneration of society. The matter became an issue in a mayoralty campaign: the winning candidate promised a firm drive to put an end to the scandal and to see that criminals were placed behind bars; the chief of police announced that he would bend all the resources of his department to the task.

But it was Hoskins who had to determine what to do with specific examples of dope using, and dope pushing, and dope transfer from wholesale suppliers to the retail level.

It was easy to pick up small-fry users, whose lives were at their dregs, and who were being bled white by the pushers, but what good would that do? For that matter, it was easy to pick up the pushers, and how much more good did that do? Even if you got them past the lawyers and the courts, the prisons were already bursting at the seams and there was no money to build new ones.

The flow had to be stopped much nearer the source and *that* was Hoskins's job.

In the course of time, he managed to work out one important method of delivery, one key item in the transportation link that affected his own city. Important deliveries, it seemed, were made by car by one particular person. Little by little, through complicated analyses of events, through information squeezed out of informers, details were filled in.

It was simplicity itself. There was no attempt to hide the material. It was in some sort of container under the driver's seat. It was simply driven from point A to point B, usually in the early dawn.

The driver was a master of simple disguise. He changed hats and hairstyle. He would wear contact lenses or horn-rims, sweaters or sports jackets, or heavy-duty shirts. He never looked the same twice, and the only thing that always characterized him was that he was never noticeable.

Nor did he ever use the same car twice; nor stick to the same route; nor to the precise points A and B.

He came to be called the Fox. It was a private name the police used, and it boiled down to a private war between Hoskins and the Fox. I suspect the Fox knew this and enjoyed it, and got more of a kick defeating Hoskins than out of making whatever profits he enjoyed.

As for Hoskins, I'm sure he would have been willing to have allowed the drug traffic free reign in the city, if he could only snare the Fox. Hoskins wasn't in it for abstract justice; he just lusted after the chance to catch this particular person.

We were sharing a drink once when he broke down and told me about it. I'm sure he didn't want to, because he was a proud man, who would have liked to snare his adversary without outside help. In the end, though, he was driven to ask for it. The need to win at any cost and in any way forced him to come to me.

"The trouble is," he said, "that bastard has second sight. I'm sure of it. There have been times when we were sure we knew which route he would take, and we would set up a roadblock at some bottleneck and stop cars and search them. We never found a thing, and by the time we gave up, the new supply of dope had been delivered. He could always sense a roadblock far enough away to be able to take an alternate route. I think if we stopped every car in the city, he would simply not move at all, or he would find the one hole we had left; or he would make himself invisible, damn it.

"It wouldn't be so bad, Griswold," Hoskins went on, "if he were using some super-clever technique, but he just drives the thing in, without any attempt at secrecy. What contempt he must have for us!"

I said, "What do you know about him?"

"Nothing for certain. We have lots of items that one informant or another has hinted at or guessed at, but we don't know how far any of this can be trusted. He's average height and there are no distinguishing marks. We could guess that. Once we were told he had a limp, not a noticeable one, but we couldn't pin it down to a particular leg. Once we were told he was color-blind by a fairly reliable stoolie, whom we never saw again afterward, so that we weren't able to get confirmatory details. Once we were told he was well educated and sounded like a college professor, but our source surely couldn't have known what a college professor sounded like."

I said, "Does he drive alone on these occasions?"

"We're pretty sure of that," said Hoskins. "He's not the type who would trust a confederate or who would willingly share his loot."

"It's just that I thought that *if* he were color-blind, he'd have trouble telling the red and green lights apart, and he might prefer to have someone else driving."

Hoskins waved his hand wearily. "No. The lights aren't quite identical even to red-green color-blind people. There's difference in tone and shading, I've been told."

"Wouldn't he have trouble in getting a driver's license, though?"

"Not at all. They don't test for color-blindness in this city."

So I thought about the matter and then, after a while, and after another scotch and soda, I said, "Can you tell when and by what route he's going to make a delivery?"

"There are certain indications; some few scraps of knowledge we have. There are times when we can make a good guess as to when he's going to make his move, and even how. But I told you, we've never caught him."

"And you could really guess at a particular route?"

"Well, even money."

"That's not bad. And you could lie in wait?"

Hoskins shook his head. "We've tried that. I've told you. We've never caught him."

"Of course not, when you have your police cars flashing their lights and blinding everyone within sight and when you have roadblocks all over the place. You have everything but neon signs lit up, saying, 'Here be the police.' "

"Well, what would you have us do?"

"Have no police cars there at all. Have nobody there."

"What good will that do?"

"You can have two or three men a couple of blocks away from a particular intersection, can't you? You can have them on rooftops with binoculars. You can have a police car or two several blocks away from the same intersection and when a particular car passes through the intersection, you can alert the police car. One would move in behind him as he passes and the other would go out in front."

Hoskins sighed. "How will we know that a particular car moving through the intersection is the one we want. If it isn't, then we will have stopped that car uselessly, and I will swear that the Fox will instantly know and change his route, or stay home."

"No," I said. "We'll have the right car. At least there's a chance we will, if he's color-blind, and if you follow my instructions in setting up the trap."

I explained, and I must say he had no trouble in understanding. But then, it was a simple notion.

We had to wait, of course, until Hoskins knew—or thought he knew—that a delivery along a particular route would be taken. We then had to stake out a particular intersection, one we felt the Fox would pass and one that wouldn't be too crowded in the early dawn.

We set up the whole thing in as inconspicuous a way as possible and Hoskins and I were eventually waiting on an appropriate rooftop. We both had binoculars.

Hoskins said, "You think it will work?"

"No charge if it doesn't," I said, "except a little trouble for nothing. And it might work."

It was lonely up there in the quiet slowly brightening gray, and certain tension grew as car after car passed through the intersection. Then, finally, while it was still half an hour from sunrise, a car, which didn't look any different from the others, stopped at the light.

I said, "There you are."

The light changed. The car moved on and was mouse-trapped. We knew we were right when the driver tried to get out and run. He didn't make it and the dope was found under his seat.

It didn't put an end to the drug problem in the city, but it put a sizable dent in it for a while. What's more, it made Hoskins very, very happy, for he had caught the Fox, and, in the end, the Fox was put away for a good number of years.

Griswold let his voice die away, but Jennings said at once, "Come on! You're not going back to sleep! How could you tell that one car from the others?"

Griswold's white eyebrows lifted. "It was a gamble, but it worked. If he *were* color-blind, his best way of telling the red traffic light from the green would lie in the fact that the red light is always on top, the green always on bottom. Just as you automatically watch 'red-green,' he would automatically watch 'top-bottom.'

"So we picked this intersection, blocked the cross-street a corner away so that no car would use it, and then reversed the light, putting the green on top. And *then*, we put it on permanent green.

"Suppose we had put it on a permanent red at the bottom. He might conceivably have gone through thinking it was green, but that would not be conclusive. Many a driver might run a red light on an almost deserted road in the early dawn. However, *no one* would stop at a green light any time, except a color-blind person who thought it was red; as he would if we put the green on top.

"When he reached the intersection, he stopped automatically at what he thought was red even with the road almost empty and no car in the cross-street. A color-blind person would probably learn to drive with particular care in this respect, particularly if he were a criminal who didn't dare be stopped for a petty traffic violation.

"We then hand-tripped the controls to turn the traffic-light red—on the bottom—and he started at once, thinking it had turned green. I was sure we had him then, and we had."

Getting
the Combination

Baranov arrived when the rest of us were already at the Union Club. He sat down with a triumphant air. "Is Griswold asleep?"

I looked in Griswold's direction and shrugged. "As asleep as he ever is."

"Well, forget him. Remember the time when he told us about solving a mystery by knowing that there was no number under a thousand which, when spelled out, contains the letter 'a'?"

Jennings and I both nodded.

"That got me to thinking. Look, there is an infinite array of numbers. Suppose you spell them out—the whole infinite array—"

"Can't be done," said Jennings. "How can you spell out every one of an infinite number?"

"In imagination," said Baranov impatiently. "Now arrange them all—the whole infinite set of them—in alphabetical order. Which number is first in line?"

Jennings said, "How can you tell unless you look at all the numbers? And how can you look at all of an infinite number?"

"Because there's a pattern to number names," said Baranov. "There may be an infinite set of numbers, but there are only a small number of ways in which their names are formed. The number first in line, alphabetically, is 'eight.' Nothing comes ahead of it. There's no number in the entire infinite array that starts with 'a,' 'b,' 'c,' or 'd,' and how do you like that?"

"What about 'billion'?" I said.

Baranov sneered at me elaborately. "That's not a number name. If you write the number 'one' followed by nine zeroes, that's not 'billion' starting with 'b'; that's 'one billion' starting with 'o.' "

And at this point, Griswold, without seeming to interrupt his soft snore, said, "And what's the last number in line?"

I thought rapidly and was the first to answer. " 'Two.' There are no numbers starting with any letter after 't,' and nothing past the 'w' in second place. The other 'tw's,' like 'twelve' and 'twenty' have an 'e' in third place and come ahead of 'two.' "

I felt that to be an excellent analysis considering that I did it so rapidly, but Griswold's eyes opened and he looked at me with infinite contempt. "You get *zero*," he said. "Let me tell you a story."

I have a friend [said Griswold] who likes to play with numbers. He's not a mathematician and has no talent for mathematics, any more than I have. Still, playing with numbers is fun even if you have no talent for it.

This friend of mine—his name is Archie Bates—used his hobby, in part, as a defense against boredom.

All of us, I suppose, have been trapped in an audience with a speaker delivering a particularly boring address, or with an orchestra playing some piece that does not grip us, or with a play turning out to be unexpectedly maladroit.

What do you do in such a case?

You might fall asleep, but that could be fraught with embarrassment if you are with others before whom you don't want to seem a clod. You might think deep thoughts, but suppose none come to mind?

Well, then, you might do as Bates would and play with numbers. He would count the chandeliers, or the lights, or the ornamental repetitions on the walls and ceilings and ring all the permutations upon the matter that he could. He found it (he frequently told me) the perfect antidote to boredom.

Or he would work up odd sequences of numbers according to some system and ask people to work out the system and predict the next number. He was never profound, you understand, but he was sometimes amusing. For instance, he once presented me with the series of Arabic digits, 8, 5, 4, 9, 7, 6, 3, 2, 0. He pointed out that every digit was included except 1, and asked me where 1 rightfully belonged.

It took me a while to realize he had placed the digits in alphabetical order, if each was spelled out, and that meant 1 belonged between 9 and 7. That was how I could so easily improve on Baranov's puzzle.

It was also possible for Bates's hobby to bring about discomfort and embarrassment, and at one time it did so.—Which brings up an important fact.

Most of the little cases I have presented you with are examples of high crimes: murder, espionage and so on. It is possible, however, to puzzle over something very small and insignificant—and even so that might annoy you and occupy your mind every bit as much as murder might. And, given friendship or interest, I have no objection to being of service in such cases, however minute in importance they might seem to outsiders.

Mrs. Bates called me one day in some agitation and asked me if I would be so kind as to come over at once. She had a problem and thought I might be able to help her. She doubted that anyone else could.

I am not proof against that kind of invitation.

When I arrived, she took me into Bates's study and showed me a safe. It was moderately large, strongly and sturdily made, and had a combination lock that included four dials, each with all the digits from 0 to 9. If each dial were turned so that the central row of the three that were exposed read some appropriate number, one to which the safe was keyed, the door would open. Otherwise it would not.

I said, "What is the problem, Mrs. Bates?"

Mrs. Bates said, "Archie got this safe last week. Why he wants it is more than I know, unless it amuses him to play with the combination. We have no valuables that wouldn't be better off in a bank vault, and we have no secrets that must be hidden away. But there it is."

"Well?"

"He has all our family records inside. I have to make out a check for something I should have made out a check for a month ago, but forgot. I have to get the check into the mail, and postmarked by midnight, or we will be involved in serious complications. The trouble is that I don't know the exact amount, or even the name and address of the people I must make it out to. Not offhand. For that matter, the checkbook is in the safe, too."

"Why is everything in the safe?"

"Because he's safe-happy, that's why. He's got the safe and he has to use it. It's *so* embarrassing."

"You've forgotten the combination, I suppose?"

"I never knew it. He never told me. I can't even call the company that made the safe, because Archie set up the combination himself."

"Why don't you telephone Archie?"

"I would, if I knew where he was. He's in Baltimore, but I don't know where. He usually writes up his itinerary and gives it to me, but this time, I think he just shoveled it into the safe along with everything else."

"But what can I do, Mrs. Bates? I don't know the combination."

She said, "There's a hint. On the floor, right next to the safe, was a slip of paper. He must have dropped it and didn't notice that he had. On it is one of those series of numbers he plays with. You know the way he does that!"

"Yes, I do."

"Here it is, then."

She handed me a slip of paper on which seven numbers were written in a vertical column: 1, 2, 6, 12, 60, 420 and 840. Underneath the 840 was an asterisk and I knew that it was Bates's habit to use an asterisk to indicate the number that was to be guessed.

"What I think," said Mrs. Bates, "is that the next number in the series is the combination to the safe. He was probably working out one of his series—you know the way he is—and that gave him the idea of making the next number, whatever it is, the combination. The trouble is I don't know the next number. If you start with 1, you must multiply it by 2 to get 2, and that by 3 to get 6, then 2 again to get 12, then 5, then 7, then 2 again. I don't know what you're supposed to multiply 840 by."

I smiled a little and said, "It doesn't matter, Mrs. Bates. Just multiply 840 by each number from 2 to 9, and then try each product. It will take you only a few minutes. In fact, if you start with 0000 and try each number in order up to 9999, you will surely open the door eventually. If you try only one combination each second, you will go through the entire list in 2¾, hours and will probably open the door within an hour and a half. Then you can make out the check. This combination system is not a very good one, you see."

Mrs. Bates looked exasperated. "Oh yes, it is. Archie explained that to me. In this make, he said, if you set any combination *except* the right one, and try to open the door, the little number things freeze and can't be moved again until they are unfrozen with a special magnetic key. Archie says that without the key the safe has to be blown open with an explosive."

I said, "And your husband has the key with him, wherever he is, I suppose."

She nodded. "That's right, so I have to figure out the correct combination right off. I just don't have the nerve to make a guess and try. If I'm wrong, then I have to call a locksmith. And even if a locksmith is willing to come right over and blow it open and I make out the check—which I should have done a month ago—the safe will be destroyed. I guess Archie would just about kill me."

"But then what do you expect *me* to do?"

She sighed. "But isn't it obvious? You're always telling Archie about all the clever ways in which you solve crimes when the police and FBI are stuck, so can't you just look at the series of numbers and tell me what the combination is?"

"But suppose I'm wrong. I may be clever but I'm not a superman," I said, for as you gentlemen all know, if I have a fault at all, it is the possession of a certain excess of diffidence and modesty.

"I'm certain you're not," said Mrs. Bates coolly. "If

you freeze it, however, Archie will have to take it out on you and what do you care?"

I wasn't at all sure that it was safe for me not to care. Bates is a large man with a hair-trigger temper. I doubted that he would actually strike his wife, though he would surely storm at her and berate her mercilessly. I was not at all sure, however, that he might not grant me less consideration, and black my eye for me.

I will admit, however, that Mrs. Bates's apparent certainty that I was not a superman rankled. *I* might say so, but I saw no reason for having *her* take the privilege. So I merely adjusted the four dials to the appropriate number, turned the handle and opened the door for her.

Then, with a rather chilly bow, I said, "Your husband will have no occasion for anger with either of us now," and left.

Griswold snorted grimly at the conclusion of the tale and sipped gently at his scotch and soda. "I suspect you all saw the proper combination long before I completed the story."

"Not I," I said. "What is the combination, and how did you get it?"

Griswold snorted again. "Look at those numbers," he said. "The larger ones look easy to divide evenly in a number of different ways. The first number, 1, can, of course, be divided only by 1 itself. The second number, 2, can be divided by 1 and 2. The third number, 6, can be divided evenly by 1, 2 and 3. In fact, it is the smallest number that can be divided by 1, 2 and 3, as you can easily check for yourself."

"It can be divided by 6," I pointed out.

"Irrelevant," said Griswold. "I am speaking of the consecutive digits, beginning with 1, that will serve as divisors. The fourth number, 12, is the smallest number that can be divided by each of the first four digits, 1, 2, 3 and 4. It can also be divided by 6 and 12, but that is irrelevant.

"You see that the fifth number is 60. It can be divided evenly by 1, 2, 3, 4 and 5; and, as it happens, by 6 also. It is the smallest number that can be divided by each of the first six digits. The next number is divided evenly by all the digits from 1 through 7, and the final number 840, by all the digits from 1 through 8.

"The next number, which would be the combination, should therefore be the smallest number that can be divided by all the digits from 1 through 9. If you multiply 840 by 3, the product is divisible by 9 and stays divisible by all the smaller digits. Since 840 multiplied by 3 is 2520, that is the combination. The number 2520 is the smallest number divisible by all the digits, 1 through 9, and, as a matter of fact, it happens to be divisible by 10 as well. And there you are!"

The Library Book

I looked about at the other three at the Union Club library (Griswold had smoothed his white mustache, taken up his scotch and soda and settled back in his tall armchair) and said rather triumphantly, "I've got a word processor now and, by golly, I can use it."

Jennings said, "One of those typewriter keyboards with a television screen attached?"

"That's right," I said. "You type your material onto a screen, edit it there—adding, subtracting, changing—then print it up, letter-perfect, at the rate of 400-plus words per minute."

"No question," said Baranov, "that if the computer revolution can penetrate your stick-in-the-mud way of life, it is well on the way to changing the whole world."

"And irrevocably," I said. "The odd part of it, too, is that there's no one man to whom we can assign the blame. We know all about James Watt and the steam engine, or Michael Faraday and the electric generator, or the Wright Brothers and the airplane, but to whom do we attribute this new advance?"

"There's William Shockley and the transistor," said Jennings.

"Or Vannevar Bush and the beginnings of electronic computers," I said, "but that's not satisfactory. It's the microchip that's putting the computer onto the assembly line and into the home, and who made that possible?"

It was only then that I was aware that for once Griswold had not closed his eyes but was staring at us, as

155

clearly wide awake as if he were a human being. "I, for one," he said.

"You, for one, what?" I demanded.

"I, for one, am responsible for the microchip," he said haughtily.

It was back in the early 1960's [said Griswold] when I received a rather distraught phone call from the wife of an old friend of mine, who, the morning's obituaries told me, had died the day before.

Oswald Simpson was his name. We had been college classmates and had been rather close. He was extraordinarily bright, was a mathematician, and after he graduated went on to work with Norbert Wiener at M.I.T. He entered computer technology at its beginnings.

I never quite lost touch with him, even though, as I need not tell you, my interests and his did not coincide at all. However, there is a kinship in basic intelligence, however differently it might express itself from individual to individual. This I *do* have to tell you three, as otherwise you would have no way of telling.

Simpson had suffered from rheumatic fever as a child and his heart was damaged. It was a shock, but no real surprise to me, therefore, when he died at the age of forty-three. His wife, how-ever, made it clear that there was something more to his death than mere mortality and I therefore drove upstate to the Simpson home at once. It only took two hours.

Olive Simpson was rather distraught, and there is no use in trying to tell you the story in her words. It took her awhile to tell it in a sensible way, especially since, as you can well imagine, there were numerous distractions in the way of medical men, funeral directors and even reporters, for Simpson, in a limited way, had been well-known. Let me summarize, then:

Simpson was not a frank and outgoing person, I recall, even in college. He had a tendency to be secretive about his work, and suspicious of his colleagues. He has always felt people were planning to steal his ideas. That he trusted me and was relaxed with me I attribute entirely to my nonmathematical bent of mind. He was quite convinced that my basic ignorance of what he was doing made it impossible for me to know what notions of his to steal or what to do with them after I had stolen them. He was probably right, though he might have made allowance for my utter probity of character as well.

This tendency of his grew more pronounced as the years passed, and actually stood in the way of his advancement. He had a tendency to quarrel with those about him and to make himself generally detestable in his insistence on maintaining secrecy over everything he was doing. There were even complaints that he was slowing company advances by preventing a free flow of ideas.

This, apparently, did not impress Simpson, who also developed a steadily intensifying impression that the company was cheating him. Like all companies, they wished to maintain ownership of any discoveries made by their employees, and one can see their point. The work done would not be possible without previous work done by other members of the company and was the product of the instruments, the ambience, the thought processes of the company generally.

Nevertheless, however much this might be true, there were occasionally advances made by particular persons which netted the company hundreds of millions of dollars and the discoverer, mere thousands. It would be a rare person who would not feel ill-used as a result, and Simpson felt more ill-used than anybody.

His wife's description of Simpson's state of mind in the last few years made it clear that he was rather over the line into a definite paranoia. There was no reasoning with him. He was convinced he was being persecuted by the company, that all its success could be attributed to his own work, but that it was intent on robbing him of all credit and financial reward. He was obsessed with that feeling.

Nor was he entirely wrong in supposing his own work to be essential to the company. The company recognized this or they would not have held on so firmly to someone who grew more impossibly difficult with each year.

The crisis came when Simpson discovered something he felt to be fundamentally revolutionary. It was something that he was certain would put his company into the absolute forefront of the international computer industry. It was also something which, he felt, was not likely to occur to anyone else for years, possibly for decades, yet it was so simple that the essence of it could be written down on a small piece of paper. I don't pretend to understand what it was, but I am certain now it was a forerunner of microchip technology.

It occurred to Simpson to hold out the information until the company agreed to compensate him amply, with a sum many times greater than was customary, and with other benefits as well. In this, one can see his motivation. He knew he was likely to die at any time and he wanted to leave his wife and two children well provided for. He kept a record of the secret at home, so that his wife would have something to sell to the company in case he did die before the matter was settled, but it was rather typical of him that he did not tell her where it was. His mania for secrecy passed all bounds.

Then one morning, as he was getting ready to get to work, he said to her in an excited way, "Where's my library book?"

She said, "What library book?"

He said, *"Exploring the Cosmos.* I had it right here."

She said, "Oh. It was overdue. I returned a whole bunch of them to the library yesterday."

He turned so white she thought he was going to collapse then and there. He screamed, "How dare you do that? It was *my* library book. I'll return it when I please. Don't you realize that the company is quite capable of burglarizing the home and searching the whole place? But they wouldn't think of touching a library book. It wouldn't be mine."

He managed to make it clear, without actually saying so, that he had hidden his precious secret in the library book, and Mrs. Simpson, frightened to death at the way he was gasping for breath, said distractedly, "I'll go right off to the library, dear, and get it back. I'll have it here in a minute. Please quiet down. Everything will be all right.''

She repeated over and over again that she ought to have stayed with him and seen to it that he was calmed, but that would have been impossible. She might have called a doctor, but that would have done no good even if he had come in time. He was convinced that someone in the library, someone taking out the book, would find his all-important secret and make the millions that should go to his family.

Mrs. Simpson dashed to the library, had no trouble in taking out the book once again and hurried back. It was too late. He had had a heart attack—it was his second, actually—and he was dying. He died, in fact, in his wife's arms, though he did recognize that she had the book again, which may have been a final consolation. His last words were a struggling ''Inside—inside—'' as he pointed to the book.—And then he was gone.

I did my best to console her, to assure her that what had happened had been beyond her power to control. More to distract her attention than anything else, I asked her if she had found anything in the book.

She looked up at me with eyes that swam in tears. ''No,'' she said, ''I didn't. I spent an hour—I thought it was one thing I could do for him—his last wish, you know—I spent an hour looking, but there's nothing in it.''

''Are you sure?'' I asked. ''Do you know what it is you're looking for?''

She hesitated. ''I *thought* it was a piece of paper with writing on it. Something he said made me think that. I don't mean that last morning, but before then. He said many times 'I've written it down.' But I don't know what the paper would look like, whether it was large or small, white or yellow, smooth or folded—*anything!* Anyway, I looked through the book. I turned each page carefully, and there was no paper of any kind between any of them. I shook the book hard and nothing fell out. Then I looked at all the page numbers to make sure there weren't two pages stuck together. There weren't.

"Then I thought that it wasn't a paper, but that he had written something in the margin. That didn't seem to make sense, but I thought *maybe*. Or perhaps, he had written between the lines or underlined something in the book. I looked through all of every page. There were one or two stains that looked accidental, but nothing was actually written or underlined."

I said, "Are you sure you took out the same book you had returned, Mrs. Simpson? The library might have had two copies of it, or more."

She seemed startled. "I didn't think of that." She picked up the book and stared at it, then said, "No, it must be the same book. There's that little ink mark just under the title. There was the same ink mark on the book I returned. There couldn't be two like that."

"Are you *sure?*" I said. "About the ink mark, I mean."

"Yes," she said flatly. "I suppose the paper fell out in the library, or someone took it out and probably threw it away. It doesn't matter. I wouldn't have the heart to start a big fight with the company with Oswald dead. Though it would be nice not to have money troubles and to be able to send the children to college."

"Wouldn't there be a pension from the company?"

"Yes, the company's good that way, but it wouldn't be enough; not with inflation the way it is; and Oswald could never get any reasonable insurance with his history of heart trouble."

"Then let's get you that piece of paper, and we'll find you a lawyer, and we'll get you some money. How's that?"

She sniffed a little as though she were trying to laugh. "Well, that's kind of you," she said, "but I don't see how you're going to do it. You can't make the paper appear out of thin air, I suppose."

"Sure I can," I said, though I admit I was taking a chance in saying so. I opened the book (holding my breath) and it was there all right. I gave it to her and said, "Here you are!"

What followed was long drawn out and tedious, but the negotiations with the company ended well. Mrs.

Simpson did not become a trillionaire, but she achieved economic security and both children are now college graduates. The company did well, too, for the microchip was on the way. Without me it wouldn't have gotten the start it did and so, as I told you at the beginning, the credit is mine.

And, to our annoyance, he closed his eyes.

I yelled sharply, "Hey!" and he opened one of them.

"Where did you find the slip of paper?" I said.

"Where Simpson said it was. His last words were 'Inside—inside—' "

"Inside the book. Of course," I said.

"He didn't say 'Inside the book,'" said Griswold. "He wasn't able to finish the phrase. He just said 'Inside—' and it was a library book."

"Well?"

"Well, a library book has one thing an ordinary book does not have. It has a little pocket in which a library card fits. Mrs. Simpson described all the things she did, but she never mentioned the pocket. Well, I remembered Simpson's last words and looked inside the pocket—and that's where it was!"

The Three Goblets

It was particularly cozy in the Union Club library that night. It always was, when it was raining hard outside. The wind whipped the rain and splattered it against the two-story-high windows, and that made the calm warmth inside seem calmer and warmer. Griswold's gentle and rhythmic snoring seemed all the counterpoint we needed.

I tried not to think of my wet raincoat in the cloakroom, and of the inevitable time when I would have to leave in order to try to locate a taxi. Sufficient unto the hour—

I stretched my legs out lazily and said, "Ever think about what a consistently bad press policemen get? Even in a society where they are clearly the stalwart wall between the law-abiding citizen and the criminal, they get hardly a kind word."

"Copper!" murmured Baranov. "Flatfoot! Cossack! Pig!"

"No, no," I said, annoyed. "Those are just names. Anyone will yell a name at anyone when annoyed. I'm talking about cold blood. Think of all the mystery writers who give all the brains and insights to dilettantes in private life—to the Sherlock Holmeses, the Hercule Poirots, the Peter Wimseys—and where are the police? Why, they're Scotland Yard bunglers, one and all."

Jennings made an impolite sound with his lips. "You're living in the past, old boy," he said. "It's quite common now to have brilliant policemen do the job. From Appleby to Leopold, we have public hirelings solving the most difficult and subtle crimes. In fact, the police procedural is now much more popular than the old-fashioned Philo Vance bit.''

I had them where I wanted them now. I said, "Not if we listen to Griswold." (And I kept one eye cocked at the sleeping figure, sitting bolt upright in his winged armchair with his scotch and soda firmly in his hand.) "He always solves the crime, while the police are helpless. That old fraud expects us to believe in his systematic usurpation of police duties."

Griswold's ice-blue eyes opened at once, as I expected they would. "This old fraud expects only fools to believe that—a post for which you qualify. The police force does its job, always has. The only trouble is that police work is routine—laborious and unglamorous routine—ninety-nine percent of the time. It is only the very occasional problem that lends itself to a flash of brilliant insight that allows the gifted individual to come into his own. For instance—"

He sipped at his drink and trailed off.

"For instance—" I insisted.

The general armory of the police in its war against crime [said Griswold] is not brilliance. It is not the arm-chair genius, weaving a chain of inexorable logic, and producing the criminal in a kind of breathtaking leger-demain, because that won't work.

For one thing, that sort of thing would never stand up in court. It works in books, where the accused will confess once he's exposed, or kill himself, but that never happens in real life. The accused denies everything, and his lawyer casts doubt on everything, and if all you've got to present to a judge and jury is brilliance, the accused will get off.

The police have to gather evidence by going from possible witness to possible witness, and trying to get statements or identifications that they think will stand up under cross-examination. They have to track down guns or documents or pawn tickets, or, for that matter, bodies, by endless searches, by combing trash cans, or dragging ponds.

It requires the concentrated and boring labor of dozens of people over weeks and months.

In fact, I'll tell you the single most important tool of police work—the informer.

You all know that our government cannot stop leaks, no matter what it does. Well, neither can the various criminal enterprises. There is always someone who will talk.

The motives? They are various. There are informers who seek revenge, who fancy themselves ill-used and are burning to get even. There are informers who could use a little extra money and who charge all the traffic will bear for the information they claim they have. There are informers who are chiefly interested in the blind eye: the privilege of continuing a life of mild crime—pickpocketing, purse snatching—knowing that the police will be tender about it, provided they are useful blabbers.

That's not glamorous either. Mystery writers who expect to use informers in their tales have to give up on brilliance and make do with violence. Usually, the informer is found dead in chapter four, and can only gasp out just enough to puzzle the detective.

Of course, sometimes—very rarely, when compared with the grand total of police work—everything fails. In that case, once in a while, they may come to me. And, occasionally, I can help with just that final piece of the puzzle, which they don't see because they are too worn out with their endless routine.

There was the case of the big diamond-smuggling flap that arose a few years ago. You may have read about it in the papers. If not, it doesn't matter; my part wasn't mentioned, you may be sure.

The police could not solve the method used to transport the diamonds. They searched desperately almost everything suspicious that came into the country, and never found a diamond.

They were small diamonds, individually not very lavish, well within the middle-class reach, but in the aggregate, thousands of carats were involved, and millions of dollars. And it was continuing in an open-ended fashion.

Finally, one of the Treasury Department agents came to me. He was very nervous about it, because it was one of the times when I was particularly on the outs with the government. I had called someone a nasty name which he thoroughly deserved, and I was placed off bounds.

I don't blame the underlings, however, so I was willing to listen to him, and to help if I could. He told me about the diamond smuggling and it seemed there had been a break in the case. As one might expect, it came about through the use of an informer.

On that basis, the Treasury knew that a package was coming into the United States—a package that carried the diamonds, either directly or indirectly—that is, the diamonds would be in the package, or information concerning the when and how of their arrival would be there. The informer had no fine details, but he was certain of the basic facts—he said—and it was going to be a *big* operation.

The package arrived at the time and place foretold. It was duly intercepted and was taken to headquarters, where it was opened (with all due precautions, I might add, in case it was a booby trap—which it wasn't).

Inside the box were three fine goblets of beautiful etched glass of delicate shape and fragile structure. Quite expensive, but declared in full, and customs paid in advance by a reputable source there was no real reason to distrust.

I said, "There was nothing else in the package? Just the goblets?"

"Just the goblets."

"No diamonds?"

"Not one."

"What did you do?"

The agent said, "Well, to begin with, we went over those goblets for anything we could find—"

"You mean the diamonds might have been added to the molten glass, so that they were now part of the goblets?"

"Not at all," said the agent stiffly. "Diamonds are carbon. They oxidize at elevated temperature, and molten glass would certainly damage them. Besides, they would show up at once on refractive index measurements and we tried that just to be thorough."

(There's the value of police work! I have no equipment to run such tests, or the expertise for doing them, if I had the equipment.)

"What else did you do?" I asked.

"There was etching on the glass. It consisted of abstract shapes and it occurred to us it might carry coded information. It didn't. We photographed it and studied those photos under a lowpower microscope. We could find nothing, no irregularities at all in the symmetry of form—and perfect symmetry carries no information."

"The goblets must have been wrapped in something. What about that?"

"Oh, yes. They were wrapped in tissue paper, several thicknesses. We took them apart and went over them carefully, each sheet, both sides. We studied them under warmth, under magnification, under ultraviolet light. Nothing showed up. We had our invisible ink experts give it the full treatment. Nothing."

"The box itself?"

"We didn't ignore it, I assure you. We went over every inch of it inside and out, as carefully as we had done the tissue paper. We even removed the tape used to secure the box, as well as the various labels and stamps, so that we could study the portion of the box underneath, to say nothing of the tape, labels and stamps themselves."

"And I presume you found nothing."

"Not a damn thing."

I thought about it awhile and said, "Has it occurred to you that your informer may be mistaken—or lying?"

The agent grimaced. "Right away. We had him in. I don't know if he has a mother's grave, but he swore on it. We find ourselves believing him."

"Perhaps you picked up the wrong package."

"It fits every detail of the informer's advance description. The chances against its being wrong are astronomical."

"How big was the package?"

"Twelve inches by nine inches by six inches, just about."

"And the goblets?"

"About six inches tall. Three inches across the opening."

"Were any of the three cracked, chipped or damaged in any way."

"No, no. They were in perfect shape."

"And do you have the package now, exactly as it was to begin wth?"

"Of course," said the agent gloomily. "We have to pass it on to the rightful owner with some lie about its having been lost or mislaid. Strictly speaking, we had no business taking it."

"No search warrant?"

"No."

"Well, don't worry. There's just a chance I may get you your diamonds."

And of course I did—in a way that you've probably already guessed. Just one of those few times when a moment of brilliance outweighs all the patient work of a crime laboratory.

Griswold took another sip of his drink and settled back in his chair.

We cried out, as one, "Where were the diamonds?"

Griswold looked surprised. "Unbelievable," he muttered. "You heard me ask the size of the box and of the goblets. Goblets of that size, placed in a box that size, would rattle around and, despite the tissue paper wrapping, would be reduced to slivers. Yet they were not cracked or chipped, though the agent specified they were fragile.

"That meant they were well packed, and these days, as you well know, the most common packing consists of light pellets of some kind of foam plastic. My own favorites are those that look like peanuts.

"In any case, the tendency is to ignore packing. You scarcely even look at it; you just get rid of it.—But I looked at it. I went through that box, looking at each of the pieces of plastic, and many of them showed signs of having been tampered with—something hard having been pushed in, and the end compressed to wipe out the hole of entry.

"We pulled all those plastic bits open, and nestling inside of a lot of them were very pretty diamonds. What a haul we made!"

Spell It!

Jennings was the last to arrive and as he sat down, stretched his legs out in comfort and accepted his usual dry martini (with a pearl onion), he said, "There are eight million stories in the naked city."

"Hey," said Baranov, "what an idea for a TV series!"

"The only trouble is that we miss them all. I probably missed one on the way to the Union Club. I always walk here on nice days. Good constitutional, helps keep me fit. Not like you, tubby," he said, addressing me.

I was irritated. "You keep fit by aerating the brain into a neat specimen of vacuum. You don't even make sense when you talk."

From his high-winged armchair, Griswold stirred, and the soft burr of his snoring was interrupted by a soft murmur. I don't know what he said; something about a pot, I think, and possibly a kettle.

I said, "What did you miss, Jennings? Usually, you're observant enough to step in every pothole you encounter."

Jennings pretended to ignore me. "I passed a young couple arguing. The girl, not more than seventeen, I should judge, said in a whisper that I just caught, 'You shouldn't have let him see the shadow.' The boy, not more than twenty, said, 'It would have been dangerous, otherwise.' "

"So?" said Baranov.

"That's all I heard because I walked on. But then I got to thinking. What shadow? Why should he have seen it, whoever *he* was, and why would it have been dangerous, if he didn't see it? What was it all about?"

"Who cares?" I said.

"I do," said Jennings. "There was something unusual there; some story of the naked city; and I'll never know what it was."

"Ask Griswold," I said. "He will reason it out and from those two short sentences build a tale of intrigue and derring-do. Go ahead. Ask him."

Jennings tried to look contemptuous at that, but I could see he was tempted. Griswold's odd capacity to see beneath the surface—

Jennings looked at the grizzled old sleeper and, as usual, when his name was mentioned, it turned out that, somehow, he wasn't sleeping deeply enough to miss it.

His scotch and soda moved to his lips. His eyes opened, he brushed at his luxuriant white mustache with the back of his left hand and he said, "I haven't the vaguest notion what all that talk about shadows was. Of course, I have in my time encountered odd little events that I could see deeply into—something where no crime of any sort seemed involved; only something odd."

"Like what?" I said, deliberately baiting him.

I have always seemed to attract confidences [said Griswold]. I suppose it is partly the dignity of my presence that allows people to feel an infinite trust in me, and partly the luminous intelligence that shines in my eyes and leads people to assume they can find wisdom on which they can confidently lean.

Whatever the case, people turn to me in trouble.

I know a man, for instance, who is a writer. If I were to mention his name, you would know him at once. Any literate American and, for that matter, any literate European, would recognize his name. That name is of the essence to the story and since it was told to me in confidence, I cannot possibly give it to you, even in the unlikely case that I thought I could rely on your secrecy. I will, therefore, call him Reuben Kelinsky, making certain that even the initials are not accurate.

Kelinsky is ordinarily a carefree individual. He has few of the stigmata of the writer. He is not harried by deadlines, nor soured by reviews, nor embittered by rejections, nor depressed by shrunken royalties, nor enraged by editorial obtuseness—to say nothing of the villainy of publishers, agents, copy editors and printers. He wrote in a facile manner, sold everything, made a good living and was a happy man.

Consider my astonishment, then, when once, while we were having lunch, he seemed distinctly distrait. He bit his lower lip, clenched his fist now and then, and kept muttering under his breath.

"What is it, my boy?" I asked in sympathy. "You seem upset."

"Upset?" he said. "I am enraged. I have been trying for three weeks to cool down and I can't seem to. It's gotten so bad, I'm taking cold showers in the morning, and it's no use. I'm so hot and bothered that I steam the cold water in no time at all."

"Tell me what happened."

"May I?" he said with a hopeful look in his eyes. "Maybe you can help me make sense out of it."

"Say on," I said.

He said, "I had obtained a very good set of Durant's *Story of Civilization* for a mere pittance and I was delighted. I had read each volume from the library as it came out, and I had always wanted a complete set. The only catch was that Volume 2, *The Life of Greece*, was missing.

"Well, you know how it is. I had lived without any of the volumes for decades, but now that I had ten of them, I simply couldn't live without the eleventh. What's more, I intended to read the entire set right through in order. I did not want to have to skip a volume and return to it, and it wouldn't take me too long to get through Volume 1, so I needed Volume 2 in a matter of a week or so. It graveled me, you know.

"I should have waited till I was back in New York where I have many bookstores that I deal with, each one of which would have been glad to help me out, but I was stuck in Washington for a few days and I just hated to have to wait. When I came across a large bookstore on my way to a luncheon appointment, I walked in on impulse.

"I was in a hurry. I had the luncheon appointment and I was used to being in 'Kelinsky country,' so to speak, when I was in a bookstore, so I walked up to a desk and said to the woman behind it, rater brusquely, 'Where do you keep your sets of Will Durant's history series?' She gestured vaguely up a circular stairway. I ran up it and found myself drowning in Tolstoi and Dostoievski.

"I called down, 'Hey, I don't see Durant.'

"She gestured again, and I moved in the direction she indicated and came across shelves and shelves of him. There was *Caesar and Christ* and *Our Oriental Heritage* and *The Age of Reason Begins* and, in fact, about a dozen copies of every single volume in the set *except* Volume 2. I wasted considerable time looking, because I couldn't believe there wouldn't be even one *The Life of Greece*.

"I ran down the circular staircase in utter frustration. I was already late for my appointment, but I was determined to get that volume. I went back to the desk and said, 'Where do I order a book?' She gestured again— she never once said anything to me, that miserable woman—and I dashed over to still another desk.

" 'I want to order a book,' I said, gasping. All that frustrated running around wasn't doing me any good.

"The guy behind the desk looked at me stonily and didn't say a word. I repeated impatiently, 'I want to order a book. I want Durant's *The Life of Greece.*'

"He made no move to get an order blank. In fact, he made no move at all. After a longish wait, he said, 'What's your name?'

"I said very distinctly, feeling that would get a little action out of him, you know, 'Reuben Kelinsky.'

"And he said, 'Spell it!'

"That did it. I felt I was in some sort of nightmare. I don't say that everyone in the world has heard of me. I don't say that I expect as many as one person out of ten, or out of a hundred, to be able to spell my name on hearing it, but I think I do have a right to expect some-one in a *bookstore* to be able to spell my name. There were probably at least a dozen of my books in that bookstore at that very moment.

"There was a copy of *Books in Print* on his desk, the 'Authors' volume, 'A' through 'K.' I opened it to the end—I know exactly where my name is—and said '*There's* how to spell it.'

"And he said, 'I'm not here to be abused. I won't take your order.'

"What could I do but leave? I was fifteen minutes late to my luncheon. I was so enraged, I could scarcely eat and what I did eat gave me indigestion. And I did *not* have my book, either actually or on order. Of course, once I got back to New York, I obtained a copy of the book at once and I have a complete set now, but my rage has never stopped. I sent an angry letter to the store, but just got back a reply to the effect that I had been unruly and abusive, and I was to take my business elsewhere. And there's nothing I can do. I just can't understand it."

He sat there and brooded about it, then he said, "You know, this is the first time I've told the whole story, and now that I've told it, I feel much better. It's like lancing a boil."

"Absolutely. In fact, you might as well forget about it. If that's the worst thing that ever happens to you in your lifetime, you are the most fortunate man in the world."

"I know. But why on earth did he ask me to spell my name?"

I said, gently, "Well, Reuben, I only hear your side of the tale. Were you by any chance unruly and abusive?"

"*No*, I swear to you. I've told you exactly what happened, word for word, step by step. I didn't scream. I didn't yell names. I felt like it, but I didn't. I was in a hurry and I may have looked annoyed and impatient, but not one impolite word escaped me."

"Don't get angry," I said, "but I'm pursuing all possibilities. You pronounced your name correctly, I suppose?"

He *did* get angry. "Come, Griswold, are you entering into the conspiracy, too? Don't I know how to pronounce my own name? Of course, I pronounced it correctly. I went to great pains to do so, because I wanted him to know who I was and to get on the ball and get the book for me. But I was stupid. I should have waited till I was back in New York."

"In that case," I said, "I think we are possibly on the track of a criminal conspiracy and I will ask you to come with me and tell your story to a friend of mine in the government." But I suppose you three see what I'm driving at.

"No, we don't," I said stolidly.

"What? Not one of you?" said Griswold.

"Not one," I said, and neither of the other two denied it.

"In that case, you'll never get any of the tales of the naked city," said Griswold with contempt. "Look, why should the man behind the counter ask Kelinsky to spell a name he obviously knew how to spell?

"One possibility, and it had to be investigated, was that it was a password of some kind. People who don't know each other, but must trust each other in matters involving great risk, *must* have a system of recognizing each other in a foolproof manner. And the passwords used must not be so out of the ordinary as to alert anyone overhearing the exchange.

"If the bookstore was being used for some criminal operation and you, for instance, want to make sure you don't pass information to the wrong person and don't like to ask right out who the right person is, here is the tactic you might use. You ask for a particular book, and when the clerk asks your name, you announce it to be that of a well-known writer: Mark Twain, Saul Bellow, Herman Melville, or, if you wish, Reuben Kelinsky.

"If the clerk is legitimate, he knows how to spell the name and takes your order; or, if it is a living author, he asks you for your autograph and then takes your order; or he may express doubt and say you're kidding. If the clerk is engaged in criminal activities, he says, 'Spell it,' a totally ridiculous request.

"And he knows that you're a fellow criminal, if you

don't act surprised at his not knowing how to spell a name he obviously should know how to spell. If you calmly spell the name, then both of you can do business. But when you grabbed 'Authors in Print,' he knew that he had the real author and in a panic, he accused you of abusive behavior and got rid of you.''

Griswold spread his arms and said, ''See!''

Jennings said, with something like awe, ''And I suppose you did investigate the place and uncovered some kind of racket.''

''Well,'' said Griswold, ''there was a drug-smuggling operation being tracked down in Washington at the time, and I thought that this might be it, but it wasn't. The truth was that the clerk in the bookstore was no admirer of Kelinsky, and had recognized him, and had decided to have a little harmless fun at his expense, and he had succeeded.—But Kelinsky is happy now, because naturally our investigation was no fun for the clerk, even though we did clear him in the end. He'll be careful with his practical jokes next time.

''And see here, I've never claimed to be right every single time.''

Two Women

It was a beautiful day outside: calm, mild and clear. The distant trees of the park could just be made out in the fading twilight and the lights in the Union Club library were taking on the golden hue that produced a warm glow within us as well. Griswold's soft, rhythmic snore was the touch that made it all seem exactly as it should be.

I speculated idly if I could make matters totally perfect by tipping the scotch and soda in Griswold's hand, and soaking his trouser leg, but common sense told me he'd wake up if I moved a fraction of an inch toward him.

For all I knew, Baranov and Jennings were having the same thought.

I said, "Do either of you ever wonder why we have to spend enormous sums on a police force when Griswold solves all crimes without budging from his chair?"

"Ah," said Jennings, "but we have only Griswold's side of it. I wonder what the police would have to say about it if we asked them."

Griswold stirred in his high-winged armchair and stabbed us with a sudden glare from one ice-blue eye. "They would say nothing at all," he muttered in his deep voice, "for I have consulted them frequently in cases where that seemed advisable."

"Oh, you did?" I said triumphantly. "You admit, then, that you can't do everything yourself?"

"I never claimed anything else," said Griswold with hauteur, "but I generally prove more useful to them than vice versa. There's a particular case in point that took place not many years ago, but I'm sure you wouldn't want to hear about it."

"Actually," said Baranov, "we wouldn't, but how do we stop you?"

"Well," said Griswold, "since you insist, I'll tell you about it."

Word gets around, of course [said Griswold], that I am a court of last resort. When things seem hopeless, therefore, and people are ashamed of going to the police and can't afford a private detective, they sometimes turn to me.

Through a chain of intermediaries too long to burden you with, I found myself consulted by a Mrs. Harkness, who sat opposite me, face blotched with tears and fingers twisting her handkerchief.

It was a matter of her daughter, with whom she had not been in contact for over a year.

"Why do you come to me *now,* Mrs. Harkness?" I asked.

"I didn't realize she was gone. She had left for Europe, you see—"

"How old was she?" I asked at once. Mrs. Harkness was a short and dumpy woman who was clearly in middle life.

"She was twenty-eight, sir," she said. "Well, she's over twenty-nine now. Thirty, next month—if she's still alive." Mrs. Harkness was suddenly too far gone to continue, and I waited.

"As I said," she finally went on, "she was twenty-eight when I last saw her, quite the grown woman, supporting herself very well as a medical artist. She had been living on her own for five years, and she was planning to go to Europe, she told me, partly on business and partly for the joy of travel. She warned me she might not have a chance to write to me.

"I understood, of course. She never was much for writing or communicating, but she was very self-sufficient, and quite able to take care of herself—financially and every other way. I didn't think I had any reason to worry.

"However, she said she wouldn't be away more than two or three months, and when over a year passed, and I hadn't heard from her, I wrote to her address in Philadelphia, where she made her home, and the letter came back. I called the apartment complex in which she lived, and it turned out she had not sublet her apartment, but had moved out and placed her furnishings in storage. I went to Philadelphia and located the storage people. She had never reclaimed the furniture, and the bill amounted to quite a sum.

"I became very panicky. I felt she was still in Europe, and I checked various airlines in the hope of finding some starting thread that would help me track her down, but there was no record of her having taken any of them. I don't think she ever went to Europe after all; either it wasn't her plan from the start, or something stopped her. She has simply disappeared off the face of the earth."

I said, "That's harder to do than you think, ma'am. Can you think of any reason she might have *wanted* to disappear?"

"No," said Mrs. Harkness sharply.

"Was she married?"

"No, but she did have a couple of young men in her life. After all, she was a good-looking woman—five inches taller than I am and slim. She took after her father's side."

"Might she have been pregnant?"

Mrs. Harkness nearly snorted. "Of course not. She was a very methodical and systematic person. Even before she went off to live by herself, she was on the pill *and* owned a diaphragm. She was not one to take chances."

"Accidents happen even to people who don't take chances—"

Mrs. Harkness said sharply, "Then, if she didn't want a baby, she would have had an abortion. This is not fifty years ago. Neither pregnancy nor illegitimacy is much worried about these days. They certainly offer no reason to disappear."

"True enough, ma'am," I admitted. "Please forgive an elderly man for being behind the times.—Let me ask you, then, to describe your daughter to me. Tell me about her habits, her schooling, anything that might give me any way of identifying her—even the name of her dentists and doctors, if you know them, and even if they treated her years ago."

Her tears began to flow again. "You think she's dead?"

"Not at all," I said as gently as possible. "I merely want as much information as I can get in order to cover all eventualities. For instance, I would like several photographs, if you have them."

It took her quite awhile to give me enough information, and then I let her go.

And I went to the police. I had to. They had files of disappearances and, what's more, had it all computerized.

The head of Missing Persons owed me a favor. Several, in fact. That didn't mean he enjoyed taking time out to help me, but he did it anyway.

"Philadelphia," he said, "and about March of last year. Five feet eight inches tall—" He muttered other facets of the description as he punched the computer keyboard. It took him less than a minute. He looked up and said, "Nothing!"

"How can that be?" I said. "She's a person. She's corporeal. She existed."

The lieutenant grunted. "Disappearance by itself doesn't mean a thing. They don't get into our records unless someone *reports* them missing. The parents never did till they came to you. There were no other relatives to do so, apparently, and no lover or friend who was close enough to notice she was gone—or to care."

I said, "How about unsolved murders? Any appearances of an unidentified body at the time she disappeared?"

"Not likely," said Delaney. "These days it's pretty hard for a body to be unidentified unless it is hacked up and key portions are hidden or destroyed. But I'll check." And after a while he said, "Only one who could even vaguely qualify and she was black. I gather the one you're interested in isn't black."

"No."

"My guess, then, is that she did go to Europe. The mother's checking of the airlines means nothing. The daughter may have gone under an assumed name, for instance, and she may still be there, or she may have died there—and, in either case, she is certainly out of our jurisdiction. Maybe the Philadelphia police—"

I interrupted. "Why on earth should she leave under an assumed name?"

"She might have been involved in something criminal, or—" Then he stopped and said, "Oh, boy!"

"What now?"

"We had an appearance in this city at the time of your gal's disappearance. Right height, slim—"

"Where is she? Who is she?"

"I don't know. *She* just disappeared, too."

I brought out the photographs again. "Is this she?"

He looked at them briefly. "Can't say. She avoided notice. She wore a wig, dark glasses, muffling clothes. It's possible she was a member of a terrorist gang. We were about to close in, when she disappeared."

"There's no indication," I said, "that the young woman I'm looking for had any political or social interests that would lead to terrorist activity."

The lieutenant snorted. "All you have is what her mother told you, and her mother has known nothing about her for years now."

"How much do *you* know?"

He wasn't listening. His lips had gone thin and he said, half to himself, "The FBI is moving in, after our force had done the work. If we can pull it off, before they can—"

"Well," I said impatiently, "what do you know?"

He concentrated on me again, with an effort. "We've gone through her quarters thoroughly. We weren't in time to get her, but when we know all the objects with which a person surrounds herself, we can't help but know a great deal about the person.

"For instance, we have a picture here of a woman

who was intensely feminine. She had an imposing battery of makeup, from hair tint to toenail polish. Would you believe she had separate polish for fingers and toes?''

I said dryly, ''Perhaps all that is not so much a matter of femininity as paraphernalia for disguise.''

''She had flowered toilet paper.''

''What?''

''Toilet paper with floral designs on each sheet. Is that for disguise? Or is it just feminine? She was methodical, too. She had an ample supply of everything. Nothing without reserves.''

''But she left without taking anything. Why was that?''

''Desperation,'' said the lieutenant grimly. ''She left only an hour before we arrived. There must have been a leak, and when we locate the leaker, he will set records for regrets.—But for now, we will have to get your Mrs. Harkness to make an identification.''

''From what?'' I asked. ''From your list of belongings?''

''Certainly. According to you, Mrs. Harkness described her daughter as feminine and methodical. That fits. She can tell us if her daughter ever used floral toilet paper or toenail polish. She can tell us if the shade of lipstick and the brand of panty hose were the shade and the brand her daughter would wear. If she gives the right answers, I may have a name, a face, and medical records to apply to the terrorist, and that will put me neatly one up on the FBI.''

I was looking over the list of belongings—clothes of all sorts, cosmetics, knickknacks, towels, shampoos, soap, canned food, cutlery, drugstore items for headaches and minor infections, combs, cotton-tipped swabs, mouthwash, pills of various legitimate sorts, foods of various kinds in the refrigerator, books listed by name and title. Clearly, nothing had been omitted. Kitchen matches and toothpicks and dental floss. Some bottles of wine but no smoking paraphernalia, incidentally—but then, young Miss Harkness did not smoke, according to her mother.

I put down the list and said, ''Lieutenant, let me stop you from embarrassing yourself—perhaps fatally—vis-à-vis the FBI. Your alleged terrorist is not my client's daughter.''

"Oh? You can tell that from the list of belongings?"

"Exactly! We are talking of two different women."

I was right, of course. Using my information, the lieutenant put the FBI on the right track, instead of the wrong, and was commended rather than laughed at. I may have consulted the police, you see, but they just ended up owing me one more. They caught the terrorist in three days and she was *not* Miss Harkness.

Griswold took a brisk swig at his scotch and soda, and then mopped his mustache with a handkerchief that was, perhaps, a shade less white than the mustache. He looked smug.

Jennings said, "Come on, Griswold. We make nothing of this, as you well know."

"Indeed?" said Griswold with affected surprise. "I told you, I believe, that Mrs. Harkness's daughter was not yet thirty, and was sexually active? Did I not also rattle off many things on the list of possessions of the terrorist and was there not an important omission?"

"What omission?" demanded Jennings.

"The terrorist seemed both feminine and methodical, yet there was not included in the list of contents of her apartment anything in the way of tampons or sanitary napkins. No woman not quite thirty with Miss Harkness's methodical character could conceivably be without an ample supply. That the terrorist lacked any at all was proof enough that she was probably past the menopause, and over fifty—and so she proved to be."

I said, "Well, then, what was the story on Miss Harkness? Did you find her?"

"That," said Griswold with great dignity, "is another story."

Sending a Signal

"Have you noticed," said Baranov, looking up from his paper, "that everyone is sending a signal these days. No one *says* anything. Everything is a signal."

Jennings, who was sipping at a dry martini languidly, said, "It's part of the thriller mentality. We're flooded with tales of espionage and intrigue and it's just impossible for us to stoop to ordinary communication. Everything is code."

"Everything is devious," I said. "We live in a public-relations world and you don't want to spoil your image. Wallace started it in his first presidential campaign. He asked voters to 'send a signal' to Washington. In other words, if they voted for Wallace they would send an unspoken signal to the effect that they were for white supremacy without actually putting that vicious view into actual words."

Griswold, who had been unusually peaceful and who hadn't even been snoring, stared at us as though he hadn't ever slept in his life. He said, rather harshly, "Surely, some of you must live in the real world. Everything we say, everything we do, every twitch of a muscle, every slip of the tongue is a signal of some sort, and always has been. You don't suppose we communicate only by formal language, do you? The wise man must learn to interpret *everything*."

"By wise man," I said sardonically, "you mean, of course, yourself?"

"I certainly don't mean one of you three," said Griswold. "I remember a case in point—"

*   *   *

It was 1966 [said Griswold] and the Department was greatly harried. I was called in by the chief, which was itself a signal (speaking of signals) of the Department's desperation, for I was never used but as a last resort. They used to say I wasn't reliable, by which they meant that I disagreed with them half the time, which was bad; that I was vocal about it, which was worse; and that I usually proved right in the end, which was, of course, the worst.

But now the chief was willing to consult me. There was, at that time, as you may recall, a gathering crisis in the Middle East, and the United States had to be very careful in its support of Israel. We were not yet dependent on Middle Eastern oil, but we were just on the edge of becoming so.

And, apparently, one of our own operatives was not to be trusted. The Arab states had a window into the heart of our policy determination, and the Department knew that the Arabs had either placed one of their own agents in the Department, or had seduced one of ours. The Department even had the code name for the agent, whether placed or seduced. It was "Granite" and the Arabs used that word in English.

"How did you find that out?" I asked.

The chief smiled crookedly. "At the moment, that is not important for you to know. Take it as given."

A code name is, of course, useful in that the side using the agent knows with whom it is dealing, while the other side does not. The other side cannot translate code name into real name. As in any code, however, there are possibilities for breakage.

The chief said, "From the nature of the information that is known to have leaked, suspicion focusses on five of our agents. It would be helpful if we could have a reasonable idea as to which it is likely to be, and quickly, too. We could put all five out of action, of course, but in that case, we rid ourselves of four good agents, and if we keep it up for long, we cloud four careers unjustifiably and produce stains that may not wipe off."

"Do I know these agents?"

The chief looked thoughtful. "Perhaps not," he said.

"As you know, you don't work very closely with us. So I will give you their names, and tell you something about each."

"Good thinking," I said sardonically. "It's hard to come to a decision on the basis of no information at all—even for me."

The chief flushed, but let it go. He said, "The first agent is Saul Stein. Father, Abraham Stein. Mother's maiden name, Sarah Levy. Wife's maiden name, Jessica Travers. Born, New York City, 1934. Attended New York University. Majored in Semitic studies. Speaks Arabic and Hebrew fluently."

I said, "I presume he's Jewish."

"Yes."

"Then doesn't it seem ridiculous to suppose he would be secretly working against Israel?"

"Not necessarily ridiculous," said the chief. "Not all Jews are Zionists. And how do we know he is Jewish, for that matter, when he may have carefully built up a false identity. It's something we're checking into, but we have to move carefully. Unjustified suspicion is exactly what we want to avoid, if we can."

"Is he circumcised?"

"Yes. So are Muslims. So are millions of Christians. He has a thorough knowledge of Judaism and is observant, but that might be part of the cover."

"His wife doesn't have an obviously Jewish name. Is she a Gentile?"

"By birth. She converted after marriage. It looks almost too good, when you stop to think of it."

I grunted noncommittally. "Who's next?"

"A woman, actually. Roberta Ann Mowery. Father, Jason Mowery, a two-term congressman back in the forties. Mother, Betty Benjamin. Husband, Daniel Domenico. Born, Fairfax, Virginia, 1938. Attended Radcliffe and majored in economics. Rather a forceful woman."

"Is her mother Jewish? Betty Benjamin?"

"*Not* Jewish. Methodist. So is Miss Mowery."

"She uses her maiden name, does she?"

"It's her legal name. She married on the condition she keep her own name."

"Has she any motive for treason? What kind of congressman was her father?"

"Absolutely clean record. Straight arrow. Still, Mowery is one of these women who's convinced there's prejudice against her for being a woman and that it's working against her at every step—"

"There is, isn't there?"

The chief cleared his throat. "Not as much as she thinks. It's really personal prejudice. She's harsh and overbearing and no one likes her, but she's a damned good agent, so we keep her on. Still, she could feel enough resentment to want to strike back. She could be that kind."

"Number three?"

"John Wesley Thorndyke. Also Methodist, as you can guess from his name. His father is a Methodist preacher, Richard Arnold Thorndyke. His mother's maiden name, Patricia Jane Burroughs. Thorndyke was born in Olympia, Washington, in 1931, and attended the University of Washington. He majored in philosophy and, for a while, flirted with the idea of entering the ministry himself. Strongly religious and devoutly interested in what he persists in calling 'the Holy Land.' He's not one of our most brilliant agents, but he has guts and he is most dependable."

"Is he so dependable that you find it impossible for him to be a double agent?"

"No one is that dependable. Suppose his strong religious emotion is enough to make him feel that it is blasphemous to have the Holy Land in Jewish hands."

"Would he feel better if it were in Muslim hands?"

"It is possible that he would like to see the region destabilized to the point where it can be placed under an international body representing all three faiths to which it is holy—we've actually had a report that he's said so at one time, advancing it as an ideal, rather than as a practical possibility—but who knows? As a double agent, he may feel that is the ideal he is working toward."

"And number four?"

"That would be Leigh Garrett, Jr. Father is Senior, obviously. His mother's maiden name is Josephine O'Connell. He was born in Concord, New Hampshire, in 1925, and attended Dartmouth, where he majored in chemistry. He works at the scientific end of things with us. His family is Catholic, but he himself is not observant."

"Any reason you might suspect him?"

"Well, he's extremely conservative and if he's not a John Bircher, he has definite sympathies with them."

"I wouldn't think," I said grimly, "that this would bother the Department?"

The chief said stolidly, "Not if it doesn't affect his work, even though we don't welcome extremes of any kind. Emotionality is not something that is useful in our work. There is reason to think that Garrett is anti-Semitic, for instance."

"It's not uncommon."

"To be sure, but the question is—is he sufficiently anti-Semitic to want to see Israel destroyed by another set of Semites, the Arabs, even though Department policy is to do what it can to insure Israel's survival. We can't be sure of that."

"Then pass on to number five."

"The fifth is an older man, Jeremiah Miller. He was born in 1908 in Minneapolis, and attended the University of Colorado, where he majored in English literature. He tried writing, but got nowhere and he joined the Department before World War II. He had leave of absence to do some fighting and had a commendable battle record. He was wounded at Anzio. His parents are dead, and he's unmarried. He's an Episcopalian and a churchgoer."

I said, "He's been with the Department for nearly thirty years, and he put his life on line in battle. Can't you eliminate him as a possibility?"

"No, we can't. He lacks the spark that is required for advancement and he has seen a number of younger men promoted over his head. In fact, we're thinking of early retirement for him, and a half-pay pension—and he knows it."

"And he resents it?"

"Wouldn't you? His parents are dead. No siblings. No wife. He's alone in the world, and there's nothing to distract his mind from any bitterness he may be feeling. Besides, there's the question of money. His pay is not high. His pension would be less. He's too old to make a new start of any kind. So it may be that he can be bought."

The chief seemed to brood a bit. "That's the trouble, you see. Each one of the five has a motive—a different motive in each case, and there's no way of determining which motive is the strongest, or which motive has been translated into actual action. Yet we have to get a handle on this, and right away. Things are moving rapidly in the Middle East and, in a matter of days, we'll have to cut out all five, if we can't narrow it down."

"And you want me to do the narrowing?"

"Yes, if you can. Study the motives and tell me which one will produce a double agent. I can make available to you all the raw data we have on each of the five—"

"Not necessary," I said. "I think you have given me all the information I need."

"I have?" The chief seemed stupefied.

"I can't be completely certain, of course, but I estimate the odds at six to one that I have the right person."

"You mean, one of the motives—"

"Forget the motives. You're so busy being a psychoanalyst that you don't stop to look at the simple things."

And, as it happened, I was right. The result was that it was Israel that caught the Arab nations flat-footed in the Six-Day War, and not the other way around.

Jennings, Baranov and I stared at each other.

"You're faking, Griswold," I said truculently. "You had no way of choosing one of the five, and you know it."

Griswold manufactured a look of surprise. "You don't see it? Surely, you understand that a code name for an agent is of no use at all if it gives the slightest hint as to the agent's identity. None of our agents would accept a code name that would give him away. In other words, if one of our agents is known to the other side as 'Granite,' the signal that that sends us is that our agent has nothing to do, however indirectly, with granite. And that's what I call 'sending a signal.'

"We know, for instance, that the agent in question can't possibly have been born in New Hampshire, which is the 'Granite State,' and that eliminates Leigh Garrett, Jr. It also eliminates Saul Stein, since *stein* is the German word for 'stone' and that's too obviously close to granite to allow the latter to be a good code name."

"Then it must be the older man," said Baranov. "The fellow who was slated for early retirement. There's no connection with granite there."

Griswold's eyebrows shot up. "I told you he went to the University of Colorado—which happens to be located in the city of Boulder."

"The woman—" began Jennings.

Griswold broke in, "She was a feminist who absolutely insisted on the use of her maiden name. Such women are popularly named after someone who astonished nineteenth-century American society by using her maiden name. She was Lucy Stone, and Roberta Ann Mowery was an obvious Lucy Stoner. That leaves John Wesley Thorndyke, and he it was indeed. Logic is logic!"

The Favorite Piece

It is not proper—it is not *done*—to sing in the library of the Union Club. I admit that. It was just that I had attended one of my Gilbert and Sullivan sessions the night before and my brain was brimming with it, as usual. So I did enter cheerfully, with a wave to the other three and a not very loud "When the night wind howls in the chimney cowls, and the bat in the moonlight flies—" in my resonant baritone.

Jennings and Baranov looked stoical, but Griswold opened his eyes and said gratingly, "What the devil is that horrible noise?"

I stopped at once and said, "Not noise at all. It is a phenomenon I like to call music."

"I daresay," said Griswold, sipping at his drink, "that you would like to call your looks handsome, too, but you will never find agreement in either case."

"The trouble with you," I said with some little heat, I will admit, "is that you are tone-deaf."

"Whether I am or not," said Griswold, "does not alter the fact that a decent respect for the memory of Sir Arthur Sullivan should keep you from desecrating his works."

Baranov said suddenly, "Don't tell me you're a Gilbert and Sullivan fan too, Griswold."

"Not really, but once—"

He paused for another sip, and we waited. We knew nothing would stop him now.

* * *

There are such things as hit men in the world [said Griswold]. Killers for hire.

They are hard to handle for they work with professional skill, and there is no way of connecting victim and killer motivationally. Too many such murders go unsolved and the police tend to be frustrated by such cases. They're especially annoyed when they are actually on the track and yet lack that little bit required to prevent a murder or trap a murderer.

It's then that I tend to be called in. Somehow, they have the feeling that even when all else fails, I will come through. I am the soul of modesty, of course, but the facts do tend to speak for themselves.

The captain said to me, "We've made considerable progress, Griswold. We're on the track of a small group of very clever—and high-priced—killers, but we haven't been able to reach the point where we can pin them to the wall before a judge and jury. Now we have a chance to catch one of them in the act, if we move quickly and—if we know exactly what to do."

"Suppose you tell me what you know."

The captain cleared his throat. "We keep the killers under surveillance, you understand, as far as we can. We have to be very careful, though, because we don't want them to *know* they are under surveillance, and with conditions being what they are these days, we have limited resources and can't do as much as we'd like."

"I take that all for granted," I said. "What is it you know?"

"A few scraps of dialog."

"Gained how?"

"Never mind how. We can't introduce it into court, but it's authentic."

I shrugged. "Go ahead."

"One of our characters entered, saying—or rather singing: 'As someday it may happen that a victim must be found, I've got a little list—I've got a little list.' The second said, 'Oh, yes?' and the first said, 'And the favorite piece. *The* favorite piece.' Unfortunately, that's it. Nothing more."

"They got out of range of the bug, did they?—Or found it?"

The captain made a rasping sound in the back of his throat.

I said, "I take it the first one was singing a bit of Gilbert and Sullivan."

"From something called *The Mikado,* I'm told. That's out of my line."

"The killers seem to have a small bit of middle culture."

"They're not your ordinary thugs," said the captain. "But they're just as deadly."

"Does the small bit of dialog help you at all?"

"Almost! We've got a modus operandi on them. At least there are two killings we think we've tied to them, each one at a theatrical performance of the kind in which there are occasional bursts of applause, and where the applause is sure to come at certain times."

"Oh?"

"No one looks at strangers during applause. You're concentrating on the stage, where the players or the performers are grinning and bowing and making gestures. If someone comes in and takes a seat during one round of applause, and leaves during the next round, no one, but no one, looks at him. No one can describe him."

"How about the people whose feet he steps all over?"

"The empty seat is on the aisle. The victim is occupying the seat second from the aisle. The killer sits down next to him. At the next round of applause, he just puts a small dart gun under his rib cage, fires it and leaves. It makes no sound that can be heard over the applause. The victim hardly feels it, I'm sure, but the dart is poisoned and in three minutes he's dead. He slumps in his chair and no one even knows he's dead till the performance is over and he doesn't get up. We know someone must have been sitting next to him at some point in the performance, but we have no witnesses who are in the least useful."

"Very clever, but surely you can find out who arranged it. Who bought the ticket for the victim and gave a companion ticket to the killer?"

"The victim buys it himself—two on the aisle, only

his wife can't go—terrible headache. She hopes she can go later and asks him to leave the aisle seat for her. He gives the ticket taker the second ticket and says he's expecting someone later. She doesn't make it, but the killer does."

"Sounds to me as though the wife hired the killer."

"We've got to prove it, though," said the captain. "Suppose we wait for someone to come in midway and take an aisle seat. If we've got a policewoman dressed up as an old lady in a wheelchair, we can then move her up the aisle next to the aisle seat two behind him. He'll be looking straight ahead because he doesn't want to flash his face in any direction where someone can study it—so he won't see her. And she won't attract undue attention anyway. Wheelchairs in the aisle aren't unusual sights in these days of equal rights for the disadvantaged.

"Then just before the crucial applause breaks out, she'll move her wheelchair up next to the killer's seat. If he *is* the killer, he'll take out his dart gun, and she'll have a real gun in his ribs, and two other policemen will be closing in. We'll have him and we'll sweat out of him all the information we can get about everyone else in the organization. That's what plea bargaining is for."

I said, "It sounds good to me. Go ahead and set it up."

"I can't," growled the captain. "I don't know who the intended victim is, so I can't trail him. I don't know what the performance is, or where it will be held, or at what points the killer will enter or leave."

"Since you told me about those scraps of dialog you overheard and seem to think it's authentic, I should think the performance in question would be of *The Mikado*."

"Even I could think of that, but it isn't. Here, let me describe what we've been doing."

The captain leaned back in his chair and glowered at me. "To begin with, we have reason to suspect the murder will be committed some time within a month and somewhere in this city. We're not a hundred percent sure of it, but ninety-five percent at least—and there's no performance of *The Mikado* scheduled any time this spring in the city or anywhere near it.

"So we thought it might be some other Gilbert and Sullivan production. They wrote a dozen—I've become an expert on those operettas, believe me. It turns out that there are three productions this month by three different amateur groups: *Iolanthe, Princess Ida* and *H.M.S. Pinafore.*"

I said, "You've got it down to three."

"Yes, but which of the three?"

"Cover them all."

The captain ground his teeth. "There are six performances of *Iolanthe,* five performances of *Princess Ida* and eight performances of *H.M.S. Pinafore.* That's nineteen altogether. Do you think I can tie up a significant portion of my bureau in that way?"

"You'll stop a murder."

"And how many crimes will take place, or go unsolved, because I've let my men be tied up? There's such a thing as cost effectiveness even in police work. I've got to cut down the possibilities somehow. That's why I need you."

"You need *me?* What can *I* do?"

"Tell me the favorite piece."

"What?"

"He said—the fellow with the 'I've got a list' song— that it was the favorite piece. I assume he's talking about the piece sure to get the loudest and most prolonged applause, which makes sense, except how can we decide which that is?"

I said, "How can I tell you? I'm not a Gilbert and Sullivan fanatic."

"Neither am I. But there's one guy in the Department who has a friend who is. I called him in."

"Good move."

"It didn't help. In *Iolanthe,* he said there's a trio about 'Faint Heart Never Won Fair Lady,' which is often a showstopper. But there's also what he called the Sentry's Solo, and the Chancellor's Nightmare, and the whole First Act finale. He says each of them has its devotees. In the case of *Princess Ida,* there's the trio

'Haughty, Humble, Coy, or Free,' or 'A Lady Fair of Lineage High' about a princess and an ape, and Gama's song about being a philanthropist. He says they might qualify. And in *H.M.S. Pinafore*, he listed a dozen songs, so help me, 'I'm Called Little Buttercup,' 'When I Was a Lad,' 'I Am the Captain of the Pinafore,' 'Never Mind the Why and Wherefore' and so on. He ended up saying there was no way of choosing a favorite piece because every person had his own favorite and they were all great."

"It sounds bad," I said.

"But I've been thinking. The person we overheard did not say, '*My* favorite piece.' He said '*the* favorite piece,' as though it weren't a question of personal preference, but something absolute. I thought about that and I decided it's not a question of straight Gilbert and Sullivan thinking. There's something tricky about this and so I might as well ask Griswold. Tell me you can think of something."

I had never seen him look at me so pleadingly in all our years of acquaintanceship. I said, "I take it you want me to tell you which one piece at which one theatrical performance will be the one the killer will attend on the basis of this scrap of dialog you overheard."

"Yes."

So I told him. It was a long chance, a terribly long one, but I couldn't resist that pleading look and, as it happened, I was right.

Griswold finished his drink, smiled at us fishily from under his straggling white mustache and said, "So you see, I may be tonedeaf, but I am quite capable of understanding a musical clue." And he then actually settled back in his chair and made as though to go to sleep.

I shouted in outrage, "There is no clue. *I* am a Gilbert and Sullivan enthusiast, and I tell you there is no way of deciding *the* favorite piece in any play."

"No way for *you*," said Griswold with a sneer, "because you thought 'I've got a little list' was a quotation from *The Mikado*. Might it not have been a play on words? Suppose you spell 'list,' 'LISZT.' The word has the same pronunciation, but it now refers to Franz Liszt, the Hungarian musician, who wrote a number of pieces of which *the* favorite is *Hungarian Rhapsody #2*. There's no question of personal taste there. It's *the* favorite. At the Philharmonic, the program on one particular night included Liszt's *Hungarian Rhapsody*. It got tumultuous applause as it always does. Under the cover of the applause, the police nabbed the killer, then broke the murder ring, saved the husband and got the wife a prison sentence.''

Half a Ghost

Most of our discussions at our Tuesday evenings in the Union Club library arise out of moral indignation. It was Baranov's turn, apparently.

"There are something like eight congressmen," he said, "who are being investigated on suspicion of using cocaine made available to them by a ring of congressional pages. Now that's disgusting."

I think it's disgusting, too, but I was feeling irritable, so I said, "Why? How many congressmen are half-drunk half the time? How many are mentally blurred with tobacco smoke? Why pick and choose between addictions?"

"Some addictions," said Baranov, "are against the law, which makes a difference—or it should do so to congressmen."

"How many of them stretch the facts to ribbons on their tax returns? That's against the law, too."

Jennings jerked his thumb in my direction. "That's Larry Liberal for you. If they don't ban tobacco because he doesn't smoke, then they might as well permit cocaine."

I said freezingly, "I happen not to use cocaine, either. I'm just trying to tell you that hypocrisy is not the answer. We either solve the social problems that give rise to drug abuse—and that includes tobacco and alcohol—or we'll just be bailing out the ocean with a sieve, forever."

Griswold's soft snore seemed to hit a knot at this point. He uncrossed his legs, blinked at us a bit, having clearly heard us through his sleep, as, through some special magic, he always did.

"Law-enforcement officers have to enforce the law, whether that helps or not," he said. "Someone else has to solve the social problems."

Jennings said, "And I suppose you did your bit."

Griswold said, "Now and then. When asked to help. Once, I remember, that involved a ghost story—after a fashion. Or half of one, at any rate." He sipped at his scotch and soda and adjusted his position in the armchair. It was clear he was going to pretend to nap a bit more, when Jennings's shoe kicked gently against his ankle.

"Oh," said Griswold, in a dismal attempt at innocent surprise, "do you want to hear the story?"

I'm not often called into ordinary police cases [said Griswold], since the necessary methods for dealing with them represent Tom Edison's recipe for genius—ninety-nine percent perspiration and one percent inspiration.

If, for instance, there is suspicion that a drug ring is operating somewhere and is getting so completely out of control that it cannot be ignored—where it is reaching into middle-class schools, for instance, or into the police stations themselves, or into Congress, as is now suspected—then the forces of the law are galvanized.

A great many people must then do a great deal of waiting, following, questioning, sifting through statements, listening to lies, staying up late, running risks—

It takes a long time, and once in a while a great deal of heroin, or cocaine, or some other drug is confiscated; various people involved in the operation are arrested and even convicted; and the newspapers have a field day.

The drugs that are confiscated, if they are properly destroyed, never find their way into human physiology. The drug dealers are taken out of circulation, for at least a while. Even so, there are always more drugs coming into the marketplace, and there are always new drug dealers arising from somewhere. As our friend here said, it has a great likeness to bailing out the ocean with a sieve.

And sometimes—most of the time—the efforts are less than spectacular. The drugs are confiscated in trivial quantities, if any, and the majestic arm of the law comes to rest on the shoulders of privates in the ranks; or of helpless and miserable users, far more sinned against than sinning.

Yet, as I said, my friends in the police department have to struggle along, doing what they can. It is their job. And if we're going to allot responsibility for the world's troubles, they should get off rather lightly—at least in most places and at most times.

I suppose that to any police officer running an investigation into drugs, there may come a time when a run-of-the-mill bit of procedure suddenly, and unexpectedly, comes to bear promise of leading to some sort of major "bust." A bit of information comes in that might, just possibly, open the road to the higher echelons in the drug trade. Quite apart from mundane considerations, such as favorable attention in the media, promotions, and salary raises, the officer may well feel the thrill of striking a blow for the forces of decency and civilization.

Usually, it is the ninety-nine percent of perspiration that gets the police to that point, and then, if they're to strike fast, and give the opposition no chance to cover up, to set up a protective shield, they may sometimes need that one percent of inspiration, and—if they are smart—that's when the police call on *me*.

The police lieutenant did just that on one occasion, about twenty years ago or so. He was an old friend of mine, and I didn't mind helping him if I could.

"Griswold," he said, holding up the thumb and forefinger of his right hand a quarter-inch apart, "I'm this far from getting on the track of something that will lead me to the central artery of the drug flow in this city."

"Excellent," I said.

"But I may not make that little bit. I'm missing half a ghost."

"What?" For a moment, I thought the lieutenant was intending some sort of practical joke at my expense, although he was notoriously lacking in a sense of humor, practical or otherwise.

He said, "We have a line of investigation that makes it quite certain that we can put our finger on someone who will serve as a perfect conduit of information to the very top."

"Grab him!" I said, for I am impatient with subtlety when the time for direct action has come.

"I can't. We only know his nickname. He's called Half a Ghost."

"You can't be serious."

"He chose it himself apparently, and that's all we've got. He's a *whole* ghost for any chance we seem to have of identifying him."

"You have no idea at all as to who he might be?"

"Yes, we have some idea. Indirect evidence leads us to suppose he's a member of the Black Belts, a street gang."

"Might not one of them turn state's evidence, suitably induced?"

The lieutenant rolled his eyes upward, as though calling on Heaven to witness my stupidity. "Get one of those petty hoodlums to sing? Not talking is the chief item in their own perverted notion of rules of honor. And by the time we broke one of them down, Half a Ghost would know we were after him and be gone."

"Take them all."

"We couldn't hold them. This isn't a police state— more's the pity, I sometimes think. And that would alert them, too. Isn't there some way you can tell us who Half a Ghost is right now, with enough certainty so that we can hope to catch him by surprise and sweep him into giving us the information we need?"

"Do you have anything for me to go on? Anything? Even I can't give you something in return for nothing."

"We suspect that Half a Ghost has something to do with his first name. Don't ask me what. A private joke of his own, I suspect. The trouble is we have the first names of the ten members of the gang who are old enough and have heft enough to be Half a Ghost, and not one of those first names means anything at all ghostwise."

"What are they?"

"Here they are, in alphabetical order."

I looked at the list: Alex, Barney, Dwayne, Gregory, Jimmy, Joshua, Lester, Norton, Roy, Simon.

I said, in disbelief, "One of them is called Dwayne?"

"He's called Bugsy for short. Every one of them is nicknamed, but one of them has Half a Ghost in addition, that's all. Which one?"

"Look," I said, "If the nickname were Rock, I would feel reasonably sure that it was taken from the name Simon. Simon means rock in Aramaic, according to the Bible, so the Apostle Simon was called Petrus in Latin, or Peter in English. Most people know that; perhaps even these two-bit hoods. If the nickname were King, I'd bet on Roy, which is the French word for king. If it were Jericho, I'd bet on Joshua."

"Why are you telling me all that? The nickname is Half a Ghost."

"Are you certain? There's no mistake?"

"Who can be certain, one hundred percent? Give it a good ninety, though."

"Are you sure of the Black Belts?"

"Another good ninety."

"Are you sure of the first names?"

"One hundred percent. We checked with the birth certificates. And Griswold, I need it fast. I need it now. Come on, look at the list."

I looked, "It's certainly nothing obvious."

"Would I need you if it were obvious?"

"Do you know anything about these individuals aside from their names? Do you know their schooling?"

"They all went to school—officially. How much they actually attended—what they listened to—I suppose they can read after a fashion. They're streetwise, though, and they're no dummies."

"Hasn't one of them had a real education? Finished high school at least. Gone to college maybe. Don't tell me which one. Just tell me if one of them has. Or if one of them is a reader and is known to go to the library—anything like that."

The lieutenant looked astonished. "Well, as a matter of fact, one of them fits that. He went to one of the city colleges for two years before dropping out. I didn't take that seriously. These days they're experimenting with taking in anyone, you know, whatever the marks. Do you want me to check his transcript?''

"Maybe that won't be necessary. Just one, you say?''

"Just one.''

"Would it be that one?'' and I pointed to one of the names on the list.

The lieutenant's mouth fell open, and he said, "Yes. How the hell could you know just from the name?''

I explained and said, "Grab him!''

The lieutenant did and what followed may not have been strictly and entirely legal—it was just before the Supreme Court got into the act—but he had his big bust. And you have to admit that, in a way, that's a ghost story.

Griswold yawned, sipped at his drink and closed his eyes, but Baranov, who had copied down the list of names when Griswold had given them, said, "Damn it, Griswold, there's nothing in this list that refers to a ghost, or half a ghost, or an education, and you can't tell us there is.''

Griswold sneered. "A ghost is a specter, isn't it? An immaterial apparition, or appearance. Well, when Isaac Newton first passed sunlight through a prism he got a rainbow of colors, an immaterial apparition. So he called it a spectrum, and we still call it a spectrum today. People who take physics in college, or even in high school, would know that. And if he had a sense of humor, as the lieutenant didn't, he would think of the spectrum as a ghost.

"The spectrum is made up of a rainbow of colors, as I said, and these colors are in a certain order. In order to memorize the order of colors, students are frequently given a sentence such as: Read Out Your Good Book In Verse. The initials stand for Red, Orange, Yellow, Green, Blue, Indigo, and Violet, though Indigo is not usually considered a separate color. It's just a deep blue, really, and is generally omitted. The initial letters representing the order of colors in the spectrum or 'ghost' are

203

ROYGBV, if you leave out indigo, and the letters in the first half of the ghost are ROY.

"If, then, Roy is the only one with any schooling to speak of, and if ROY represents Half a Ghost, after a fashion, what else do you need?"

There Was a
Young Lady

Jennings rustled his newspaper, a practice not quite in keeping with the somber splendor of the Union Club library, and that was quite sufficient evidence of his outrage.

"Five horses killed in the latest IRA bombing in London," he said. "They knew horses would die. Why should horses have to pay for human passions?"

"They always did," said Baranov phlegmatically, "as long as there has been cavalry. Do you know how many horses died in the charge of the Light Brigade?"

I said, "As long as human beings divide themselves into groups marked off by trivial cultural differences and consider these differences worth dying for—"

Baranov cut me off, as he sometimes does when I try to put things in clear perspective, and said, "That's been going on for five thousand years of written history. How do you stop it?"

Jennings rustled his paper again and muttered, "Israel in Lebanon, Iran in Iraq, rebels in El Salvador and Honduras, terrorists everywhere—"

I said, "A decent concept of human unity against the forces of ignorance and misery, the *real* enemies—"

"And meanwhile?" said Baranov.

Griswold, who had been slowly, and with some difficulty, trying to cross one leg over the other even while, to all appearances, fast asleep, now growled softly and said, "Meanwhile you do what you can on a case-by-case basis."

"As you have done, no doubt," I said with as much sarcasm as I could manage.

"In my own small way—now and then," he said, opening his eyes and glaring at me.

The trouble spot most embarrassing to the American government [said Griswold] is Northern Ireland. Great Britain is our closest ally, and yet there are many politically active and very articulate Irish-Americans within our borders. It is impossible for the American government to make any sort of move toward one party without giving insupportable offense to the other. Even pious wishes aren't safe.

Therefore, although it is well-known that the Irish Republican Army gets much of its financing and its arms supply from the United States, there is nothing much our government can do about it openly. Great Britain is, of course, aware of this and, unofficially, quite bitter about it, and our government has to do what it can to cut down the aid—but not openly; never openly.

The head of the Department didn't have to explain any of this to me when he came to call at my diggings one evening after dinner. I understood the situation.

"There's a new weapons conduit," he said, "running from here to Ireland, and we've got to close it down. We can't condone terrorism for whatever reason."

"Is the Irish government helping?"

"Not openly," he said.

I nodded. That was not hard to understand, either. Ireland did not want the troubles to spill over the border into its own quiet land, so it had to do what it could to defuse the IRA hotheads, but it could not—simply could not—openly appear to be allying itself with the one-time British overlords against those who were fighting to free the whole island.

"I take it," I said, "you haven't been able to plug the conduit, and are coming to me for help."

The head said stiffly, "I came to show you this," and he unfolded a piece of paper.

There were five lines of Xeroxed writing on it which went:

There was a young lady named Alice,
Who said, "I don't want to seem callous,
    But I can't abide hicks
    From the big-city sticks
Like Los Angeles, Houston, and Dallas."

Some of the letters had curlicues added and, around it, were vague doodlings.

I said, "Not bad. I presume the writer was from the Northeast or Midwest?"

"Boston."

"And was expressing his or her contempt for the big cities of the Sun Belt. Its people were hicks just the same."

The head shrugged it off. "That doesn't matter, Griswold. The important thing is that this was written by one of our agents, a young fellow who infiltrated the IRA arms network. We have good reason to think he had worked out the details of the conduit."

"And there's some reason you can't ask him?"

"Reason enough. He's dead."

"Reason enough," I agreed. "Where did you find this?"

"In his hotel room. It was written the last night of his life. We are quite certain of that, and a chain of convincing circumstantial evidence seems to tell us it must have been written during a conference with the people managing the conduit. Three hours later, or thereabouts, our agent was killed in his sleazy hotel room."

"By an intruder having nothing to do with the case, perhaps."

"We don't think so because we don't believe in coincidences. The room was hastily ransacked, and presumably effectively, too, for in our own search we found nothing to help us—except, just possibly, that verse I showed you. The paper was folded up small and was under the old-fashioned bathtub-on-legs. He may have tossed it there when he realized his friends had tumbled to his identity and were at the door."

"And he thought it would help you? How?"

"He was an inveterate doodler. We know he was.

And he had the habit of being spurred into it by something he saw or heard. He wasn't even aware of it. Our guess is that in the discussion of the conduit some mention was made, let us say, of 'Alice of Dallas.' Struck by the rhyme, he wrote the verse."

I thought about it awhile. "Alice of Dallas? What good is that? Dallas, as the verse says, is a big city, and the Alices in it may well amount to thousands. It is not an uncommon name."

"You're perfectly right," said the head, "but we don't work completely blind, you know. We have independent leads and areas of suspicion. We can narrow the field immensely in our search for an Alice of Dallas. Still—we found nothing at all. There was no Alice showing up in a place or under conditions where we could see at once that we were peeping inside the conduit, or even possibly peeping."

"Are you sure you would be able to tell?"

"Yes," he said uncompromisingly.

"Does that complete the story?"

"No. Our agent mentioned three cities. We had to consider the other two."

"Los Angeles and Houston? They're even larger than Dallas. And what becomes of the Alice of Dallas that sparked this piece of elegant poetry, if that's the case?"

"It might not have been a direct spark. There might have been a remark about 'Alice of Houston,' say, and our man might have unconsciously thought, 'If it had been Alice of Dallas, it would rhyme,' and that would get him started."

"I suppose you put Los Angeles and Houston through the wringer, too, then?"

"Of course. As it happens, none of those cities are centers of IRA support, which simplifies the problem a bit. If it had been New York or Boston, we'd have had a much harder time."

"Did you find anything in Los Angeles or Houston?"

"Nothing."

"It may be the verse means nothing, then."

"We can't believe that. Our agent tossed it under the bathtub. He clearly felt that even if he had written it as a thoughtless doodle, it held something important for us. Why can't we find that, then?''

I said, "Was there anything on the back of the paper?"

"Nothing."

"Any signs of—"

"No invisible ink, if that's what you're getting at. How the devil would he be sitting at a conference, scratching away with invisible ink? As it is, it may be his doodling on this occasion in this way that roused suspicion against him."

"What about the curlicues on the letters, and those other markings on the paper? Any significance there?"

"We couldn't find any. See here, can you?" He held up the paper before my eyes.

"No," I admitted. Then I said, "You know, it's quite possible the doodle means nothing at all. He just wrote it for no reason, found it in his pocket when he got to his room, scrunched it up, tossed it at a wastepaper basket and missed. It rolled under the bathtub, but it remains meaningless. Isn't that possible?"

The head looked annoyed. "Of course it's possible— but we can't chance it. If a flood of new arms reaches the IRA from America, the British will lean hard—though quietly—on the American government. And our government will lean hard—and not so quietly—on us. I don't want to earn a black eye for the Department, and I certainly don't want to lose my job over this."

"What are you going to do, then?"

"The only thing I can do, for now, is to go over those three cities again and again. In fact, we haven't actually stopped sifting, but I need a new lead. There must be something in this doggerel that we're missing. There must be some information it's giving us which we don't see. There's something about 'hicks' or 'big-city sticks' that is meaningful, but I just don't know what that can be. Do you?"

I looked at the piece of paper again. "Are you expecting me to see at a glance something the whole Department has failed at?"

"Can you?"

I said, "Would the name of a fourth city do?"

"What are you talking about?" He snatched the paper back and stared hard at it. "Do you mean some of the letters of the words run together to give the name of a city."

"Not that I noticed," I said. "It's a good deal more obvious than that."

"I don't understand you at all."

So I explained. He stared at me, snorted and said, "Ridiculous!"

"Take it or leave it," I said. "It's all I can suggest."

He stamped out, and he never did let me know what happened; and I, of course, would not do him the favor of asking. However, I do have my friends in the Department, and I do know for a fact that no shipment of arms went through at that time. I suspect, therefore, that the fourth city was indeed the one in question, that someone named "Alice" or perhaps code-named "Alice" was located there. I had, I presumed, actually penetrated the core of the problem and helped puncture and break up the conduit.—Which did not surprise me, of course.

Griswold finished his drink with an insufferable air of self-satisfaction on his face.

"Why do you look puzzled?" he asked.

"Not puzzled," said Baranov. "Amused. This time you've just flipped off the deep end."

"There is no fourth city mentioned in the verse," said Jennings.

"As you well know," I said.

"I never said it was *mentioned*. I just asked the head if a fourth city would do."

"What fourth city?" I demanded.

Griswold said, "What I was presented with was not just a verse, or doggerel, or a stanza of poetry. It was a *limerick*."

"Of course," said Jennings. "We all know that."

"And 'limerick' is not just the name of a verse form. It's the name of a city in Ireland, an important port in the Southwest at the mouth of the Shannon River. The name of the verse is derived from the name of that city, though the details are a little obscure. If the agent heard talk of an Alice who played an important role in the conduit in the city of Limerick, he might easily have been moved to construct a limerick about Alice. And, apparently, that was what really happened.''

Afterword

I had a sneaking feeling that when I brought in "There Was a Young Lady" and told Eric that I now had enough stories to put out a full-sized collection, that he would heave a sigh of relief and say, "Thank goodness, now you can stop doing them for us."

It seemed to me that if he did, I would feel a little hurt, but I would recover quickly. After all, thinking up a new "Griswold" the first week of every month is a chore. It isn't as if it's *all* I have to do.

However, Eric *didn't* say that. What he said was "That's nice!"

So I said, "Are you getting tired of these, Eric? Do you want me to stop?"

Whereupon he looked surprised and said, "Of course not. Why? Are *you?*"

Well, what could I say? I have my pride. I said, "No, of course not! Tired? Of thinking up a new mystery every month? Don't be silly. With a dozen or so books under contract, what else have I got to do?"

So I suppose I will keep on, and in two and a half years, always assuming it doesn't kill me, I'll have thirty more stories.

I just thought I'd warn you.

About the Author

Isaac Asimov is the author of books on subjects ranging from Astronomy to Zeus. He is the author of I, ROBOT, THE FOUNDATION TRILOGY, and FOUNDATION'S EDGE. His previous mystery books include MURDER AT THE ABA and TALES OF THE BLACK WIDOWERS.